ARMORED ANGELS ALLIANCE

Daniel Duvall

Printed in Victoria, BC, Canada.

ISBN: 978-1-4269-2647-1 (sc)
ISBN: 978-1-4269-2648-8 (dj)

Library of Congress Control Number: 2010905422

*Our mission is to efficiently provide the world's finest, most comprehensive book publishing
service, enabling every author to experience success. To find out how to publish your book, your
way, and have it available worldwide, visit us online at www.trafford.com*

Trafford rev. 05/17/2010

Trafford
PUBLISHING® www.trafford.com

North America & international
toll-free: 1 888 232 4444 (USA & Canada)
phone: 250 383 6864 ♦ fax: 812 355 4082

To my parents Jesse and Evelyn Duvall

&

to my daughters Tiffany and Jennifer

"Behold, I stand at the door and knock. If anyone hears My voice and opens the door, I will come in to him and dine with him, and he with Me. To him who overcomes I will grant to sit with Me on My throne, as I also overcame and sat down with My Father on His throne."

Revelation 3: 20 & 21

PREFACE

This is a story about five close friends who form a bond with one another. They realize that everyone is born with a sinful nature. It is their desire to be there for one another, especially in times of great need.

As they step out into the fallen world, they are surrounded by the spirit of the enemy. They know that in order to conquer this foe, they must put on the whole armor of God.

These five born again Christians must battle the forces of evil as they set about spreading the gospel to the lost souls that they encounter, everyday.

The sinfulness that is depicted in this story is not sugar coated. Sin and it's consequences are very serious issues and should not be dealt with lightly.

Many people continue to wander through the wilderness of life. They stumble around in the dark completely blinded by their own rebellious natures.

Jesus Christ is the beacon of light that directs our path to lasting peace and happiness. Our sins may have nailed Him to the cross, but It was God's love that paved the way toward forgiveness.

The penalty for sin is death. Jesus died for our sins. On the third day, He rose from the dead. He ascended into Heaven where He sits on the right hand of the Father.

Jesus promises that He will return someday to judge and rule over us. His return will be when we least expect it. We must be ready and help others to learn the truth so that they will be ready when the appointed time arrives.

CHAPTER ONE

A VISION

Lake Erie was calm on a slightly cool evening. It was in the Autumn of 1996. On one of the many shores in Northeast Ohio, the Church of Faith in Christ's singles Bible study was drawing to a close. Several gulls swooped overhead, and off in the distance, several children were tossing a bright red and blue frisbee back and forth.

The lingering smell of burning charcoal filled the air, as Denise Washington smiled at the others.

Stepping proudly, over to Adam Harrison, a tall dark haired man with a slight beard growth and a full mustache, Denise placed her arm inside of his, while searching the eyes of each and every person gathered before her. She announced, "This will be the final Bible study that I will be teaching. Adam and I are getting married next month, as you all are well aware of."

Adam grinned broadly, as the group offered up their individual congratulations to the couple.

After several moments passed by, a young woman with long blonde hair, asked Denise, "Who'll be your replacement?"

"Samantha," Denise explained, "that will be entirely up to Pastor Mark. He says that he will be approaching someone that he feels will be interested. He belongs to another church, but, it seems that this man has been growing uncomfortable with this church due to it's lack of congregational support."

"Well, Denise," a young slender man, with wavy dark hair, held out his hand toward Adam and his future bride, said, "I must tell you, that I, for one, have truly been blessed by your classes."

"Thank you, Scott," Denise smiled, shaking the young man's hand, "you all have truly been a blessing to me, also."

Adam shook everyone's hands, warmly, as he explained, "Well, Denise and I have an appointment with Pastor Mark, early in the morning. We really must get going."

After everyone said their good-byes, the group watched with glad spirits as the ecstatic couple made their way, arm in arm, up the beach, toward the stairs that led to the parking lot.

Samantha was the first to break the silence, "I really feel God intends for us to do more than just live good and moral lives, attend Bible studies, listen to Christian music instead of secular music and so on....."

"I agree with you," Valerie, the young woman sharing a beach towel with a man, who was holding a guitar, said as she brushed her auburn hair from her eyes.

"What are you suggesting, Samantha?" Scott asked, as he ran his right hand along the sand beside his towel.

"I don't know," Samantha began, "I think that we should form some sort of support group. The Lord knows that it's pretty tough out there. I think that we, as Christians, should be there for one another, especially during times of trials and tribulations."

"Have you prayed about this, Samantha?" The man with the guitar asked, as he softly strummed a chord on his instrument.

"Yes, Lincoln," Samantha replied, eagerly.

Valerie smiled over toward Lincoln, as he played another couple notes, and then she commented, "I believe that we should, as Christians, go even further. I believe that God wants us to go beyond helping each other cope with everyday life. I think He wants us to go forth and help those people we encounter in our everyday walk."

Scott sat straight up and almost shouted, "I've been dealing with that very same issue. I see it as how we all come from different backgrounds, and we each deal with totally different sorts of people in the secular world, that we each have our own missions to spread the gospel in different directions. We'd sort of be like a tree trunk with branches spreading out every which way."

"Exactly!" Samantha shouted.

Lincoln stopped strumming his guitar, as he turned toward the man seated across from him. "What do you think, Chris?" Lincoln asked. "You're the only one who hasn't spoken up, yet."

Chris replied, "I think it's great, but I have to emphasize the importance of Samantha's original idea. We simply must be there for one another, when we stumble along. Because, if we are backsliding and suddenly find ourselves living lives that are not pleasing to God, then we will be defeating the whole purpose."

"Right!" Scott agreed. "We need to be able to pick each other up when we fall. Those people, who we are attempting to bring into the fold, will be scrutinizing us very closely, for we are to be living examples of how Jesus Christ wants us to be."

Valerie giggled, "We could be like guardian angels over one another."

Scott smiled, and said, "We should always be ready for anything, because Satan will throw all kinds of obstacles in front of us. We should, each of us, put on the armor of God, before we step out."

Samantha concurred, "That means we should be in constant prayer, not only for one another, but also for the people that we encounter."

Lincoln stood up, placed his guitar down upon the beach towel, and said, "We should form some sort of united front, here and now."

Chris stood up and placed his hand upon Lincoln's outstretched hand, and said, "Let's form an alliance."

Samantha, then stood up and placed her hand upon Chris' hand, and said, "Let's call it an Alliance of Angels."

Scott stood up and said, "Let's call it the Armored Angels Alliance."

After Scott placed his hand upon Samantha's, Valerie joined them. She smiled as she placed her hand on top of the others. Giggling, again, Valerie said, "The triple A's for short."

Looking toward heaven, the five young people lowered their combined hands, and then slowly raised them upwards, shouting, "Praise.......God.......!"

As Adam helped Denise into his small compact car, he laughed, as he commented, "I'm going to miss all of those Bible studies."

"Well," Denise said, before Adam closed her door, "we can always join another Bible study. One with old married couples."

Adam laughed, loudly, as he gently closed the passenger door.

Once inside the car and seated, comfortably, behind the steering wheel, Adam looked over at his future bride. For one split second, he thought he noticed an eerie glow surrounding her.

"What are you staring at, Adam Harrison?" Denise asked, with a smile.

"Oh," Adam sighed, "only the most magnificent gift that God could possibly give me, that's all."

Teasingly, Denise whispered, "Please...."

As Samantha and Scott gathered their towels up, they shook the sand from them, and watched as the others made their way up the beach.

Samantha started to wipe away some tears that were forming in her eyes.

"I hope that those are tears of joy, Samantha," Scott said, as he folded his towel in a haphazard fashion.

"Incredible tears of joy!" Samantha replied, as she gave Scott a hug.

"So," Scott asked, after Samantha removed her arms from around his neck, "where are you headed, this evening?"

"I feel this need to go and visit my mother. She's been acting a little strange, lately."

Scott nodded, and said, "I've got somewhere to go, too."

"Oh, where?" Samantha asked, as they walked toward the parking lot stairs.

"It's rather personal," Scott explained.

"Scott!" Samantha warned, "You mustn't shut any of us out like this. It could be dangerous."

"I'll be fine," Scott assured his friend, "it isn't anything that I can't handle on my own."

"But," Samantha reminded him, "you won't be on your own, from now on. You'll be taking with you all of our prayers, and you know that God is always the great observer."

"You're right, Samantha Taylor," Scott laughed, a bit uneasily, "as usual."

As Adam turned on his headlights, he glanced over toward Denise, and asked, "Do you have to go straight home, tonight?"

Denise asked, as Adam backed his car out of it's parking space, "What did you have in mind, Mr. Harrison?"

Adam made his way toward the main road that ran along the lake shore, and replied, "Oh, I just thought maybe we could stop off at Franklyn's Diner and have ourselves a little bite to eat."

"You, my future husband," Denise laughed, "are a bottomless pit."

"What can I say?" Adam laughed, as he pulled out onto the road.

Valerie stopped abruptly, and fell to her knees. Her hands were trembling and tears began to fall down her cheeks.

"What is it?" Lincoln asked.

Chris explained, "Valerie sometimes has these ah...premonitions."

"Premonitions?" Lincoln asked. "Of danger, or something?"

"I don't know," Chris replied, as he knelt down beside Valerie and placed his arm around her slender shoulders.

"Sometimes, I think of it as a curse," Valerie cried, as she rocked back and forth.

"A curse?" Lincoln shouted. "I would think, that if this second sight came from God that it naturally would be a gift."

"It is a gift," Valerie admitted. "But sometimes, I can feel things so sensitively, that it can really hurt."

"What are you feeling, now?" Chris asked, while attempting to massage Valerie's trembling shoulders.

"It feels like someone is in danger. It feels like someone out on the streets tonight, doesn't belong behind the wheel."

"Maybe we should hold off, before we get into our cars," Chris suggested.

"How often has she been right with these...these...premonitions?" Lincoln asked, as a chill began to run down his spine.

Chris glanced over toward Lincoln, and with all sincerity, replied, "She's never been wrong, yet."

Adam turned on the radio and flipped a cassette tape into the player. The sound of Ray Boltz filled the car.

Denise commented, "Ray Boltz will be performing here in October."

"Maybe we'll get a chance to go see him," Adam said, while a song was just finishing up.

Denise reached down to get her purse. Adam glanced over and asked, "What's wrong?"

"Oh, nothing," Denise replied. "I think that I might have a schedule of concerts in my purse. I'm trying to find out the exact date of this concert."

"I think it's October 21st," Adam said.

"Great!" Denise commented. "Maybe we can take my sisters along."

As Samantha and Scott caught up with the others, they found the three of them in fervent prayer.

Seeing that Scott was about to interrupt, with a question, Samantha whispered, "Sh....," as they moved on, silently.

Suddenly, Valerie looked up and shouted toward Samantha and Scott, "Hey! Wait a minute you two. There's something dangerous out there."

Chris ran after the two as they began to ascend the stairs.

After catching up with them, Chris explained, "Valerie has had another one of her premonitions."

Scott commented, skeptically, "Chris, you know how I feel about Valerie's so-called premonitions. They border on the occult, you know, like tarot cards and such. I put about as much credence into her premonitions as I would into those people who make millions of dollars bilking people with all their phony claims to having psychic powers."

"Scott," Chris warned, with a deep serious tone, "this one was incredibly strong. It almost rendered her totally paralyzed."

Scott replied, "I'm not so sure, if this...gift...of hers is from God or from the devil."

"Believe me," Samantha interceded on Chris' behalf, saying, "it's from God. Valerie once warned me about going to church along the usual route that I always took. Well, it just so happens...that if I had traveled that road, on that very morning, I could have been killed."

"What happened?" Scott asked, skeptically.

"A gas line exploded, for no apparent reason. It took out the entire street."

Samantha nodded, as Chris went on to explain, "It occurred, precisely, at the very moment, that Samantha would have been passing through there, as was always her routine."

"A coincidence?" Scott asked.

"I hardly think so!" Samantha replied.

Denise glanced out of her passenger side window, and noticed the bright orange sunset, as it appeared, between a row of trees.

"That...is truly beautiful!" She commented.

"It's another one of God's greatest gifts to us," Adam agreed. "Just think about all of the couples all over this world who have fallen in love with each other, while watching the sun set."

"You are truly a romantic, Mr. Harrison," Denise laughed, as she continued to look out of her window.

Valerie, slowly rose up from the ground, brushed the sand from her clothes, and apologized to everyone, "I'm sorry. I never know when I'm going to get one of these...these...premonitions."

"Do you think that one of us here is in any kind of danger, Valerie?" Samantha asked.

Valerie, nervously, looked around, and replied, "I'm not sure! The feeling is getting weaker."

Scott stepped over to Valerie and said, "Perhaps, that is the blessing."

Valerie lightly punched Scott on the right shoulder, and said in a teasing manner, "Oh, ye of little faith."

Lincoln announced, "I'm going to walk along the beach for awhile. Would anyone care to join me?"

"I'm sorry, Lincoln," Samantha explained, "but I'm going over to see my mother. She hasn't been herself, lately."

Chris replied, "I think that I had better drive Valerie home. She's still pretty shook up. We can pick her car up in the morning."

Lincoln turned toward Scott, who said that he he was going somewhere, and that he didn't have much time to get there.

Lincoln teased, "For a newly formed alliance, we sure are all going off in different directions, right away."

Samantha apologized, once again, as she headed for the parking lot, followed by Scott and then, by Chris and Valerie.

Lincoln, while still holding his guitar, watched as his friends disappeared up the stairs. A cool breeze suddenly began to blow. Lincoln zipped up his blue suede jacket and turned up his collar as he started down the beach.

While waiting at a traffic light, Adam asked Denise, "Honey, who have you finally decided to ask to be your maid of honor?"

Denise replied, with a smile, "I've asked my sister Rosalie. She's so excited."

Adam smiled, and said, "I like Rosalie. I think you've made a great choice."

"Is Denny going to be your best man?" Denise asked, as if she already knew the answer.

"How did you guess?" Adam laughed.

"Could it be that you two have been the best of friends ever since the two of you could remember?"

"Elementary, my dear!" Adam laughed as the light turned green, and then he proceeded, cautiously, through the intersection.

Scott could not shake the image of the young boy he saw wandering the streets late last night. He reminded Scott of himself, at that age. The boy was asking for nothing but trouble, but like Scott, he was not aware of it.

As Scott got into his car, he recalled the short conversation that he had with the boy. He had asked him, "Why are you roaming the streets this late at night?"

The boy, a thin boy with lots of wavy blonde hair, which lie beneath a blue and white baseball cap, replied, "Because, my mother's boyfriend is spending the night again, that's why."

Scott could feel the boy's pain, as he listened to every word.

"When will you go home?" Scott had asked the boy.

The boy replied, "When I see that red truck out of our driveway, that's when it'll be safe to go home."

"What's your name, Son?" Scott had recalled asking out of genuine concern.

"Why do you want to know?" The boy asked suspiciously. "Are you some sort of weirdo?"

Scott rushed quickly to his own defense, and answered, almost awkwardly, "No, I'm not some sort of weirdo. I just simply asked you what your name is, that's all."

"It's Shaun, as if it makes any kind of difference," the boy answered, rather rudely.

The image of the boy walking off into the night, alone and depressed, just about wrenched Scott's heart to pieces, as he recalled his own nightmarish past alone on the streets late at night.

Scott started up his car and headed off toward the highway.

Lincoln began to strum his guitar as he walked down the sandy beach. The darkness was quickly enveloping the shore, as he softly sang a tune. The memory of his sweet grandmother singing to him and his brothers suddenly came to Lincoln. He smiled, as he recalled her sweet voice singing about the goodness of Jesus Christ.

Lincoln thanked God for his grandmother, as he vowed that he would visit her more often instead of taking her for granted like he had been doing, lately.

Becoming lost in his thoughts, Lincoln was unaware that he was being followed by two burly figures, who were drinking out of paper bags, swaggering and leering.

As Samantha started down the highway, she immediately noticed that a car had suddenly appeared from behind her. The car was now following too closely. She glanced into her rear view mirror, winced at the bright lights, and started to panic a little.

Samantha quickly turned on the radio. She heard a preacher saying a prayer.

Concentrating on the preacher's voice, Samantha tried to ignore the car behind her.

Once Chris and Valerie found themselves on the highway, Valerie had another one of her premonitions, as she whispered, "There's going to be an accident on this street, tonight. I feel it even stronger, now."

Chris gripped the steering wheel even tighter. He glanced into his rear view mirror, saw nothing out of the ordinary, breathed a temporary sigh of relief, and then continued, cautiously, down the highway.

A red car pulled out of a local tavern. The driver was sitting extremely close to the steering wheel, as if they were having difficulty seeing up ahead. The car made a sharp turn onto the main road. It's tires squealed loudly. As the car took a position on the road, it began to swerve. Eventually, the driver became able to control the car, and to keep it, relatively, off the median strip.

Lincoln turned suddenly, as an arm rested upon his shoulder. The smell of liquor permeated Lincoln's nostrils, as the two huge men hovered over him.

"Why don't you and your kind go back to where you came from, Boy?" One of the men asked, as he grinned, revealing to Lincoln, a complete set of yellow stained teeth.

Becoming completely repulsed at both the sight and the smell of these two men, Lincoln attempted to just walk away, when the other man laughed, "Lou, I do think that, Guitar Man, here, thinks you're nothing but a fat, old, dirty bigot."

"Is that what he thinks, J.T.?" The first man laughed, while grabbing Lincoln's guitar from him.

"Give that back to me!" Lincoln demanded.

"He speaks, Lou," J.T. grinned, revealing another set of yellow teeth.

"Here," Lou snickered, "let me entertain you, Kid. I used to listen to the Grand Ole Opry. I can play as good as any one of them."

Lincoln grimaced as he watched the man begin to play with his guitar.

When Lincoln began to wrench the instrument away from the man, J.T. quickly knocked Lincoln to the ground, forcing the wind from his lungs.

As Lincoln struggled to regain his breath, Lou, accidentally, broke a string.

Lincoln watched, in horror, as his guitar was flung to the ground, and watched as the man was about to step on it.

Suddenly, from somewhere off in the distance, a voice was heard shouting, "What's going on over there?"

Lou and J.T. turned on their heels, dropping their bags to the ground and ran up the beach like a couple of scared rabbits.

After the two men left, Lincoln regained his composure, crawled over to his precious guitar, and then he looked off in the direction of the voice that had intervened in his behalf.

To Lincoln's surprise, he saw absolutely, no one.

Samantha decided to pull slightly over to the side of the road, hoping to indicate to the driver of the car behind her, to pass her up.

The car, however, did not oblige. Instead, the car continued to follow her at a dangerously close proximity.

The memory of Valerie's words kept going through Samantha's mind, as she glanced periodically, at the car behind her.

Samantha decided to take an unscheduled turn down a side street. Without advanced warning, she quickly veered her car down a stony street, kicking up stones and dust in the process.

After making the abrupt turn, Samantha felt her heart beat rapidly, almost as if it were going to beat right out of her chest. To her delight, Samantha realized, as she looked through her rear view mirror, that she had, indeed lost her tailgate.

Coming to a complete stop, Samantha turned the engine and the headlights off, until she could calm her nerves back down.

"Thank you, Lord!" Samantha whispered, breathlessly.

Adam glanced over toward his bride to be, and smiled. Denise had just settled back in her seat, and fallen asleep. To Adam, Denise looked to be completely at peace, as she silently slept.

She never looked more lovely, Adam thought. "Thank you, Lord," Adam whispered under his breath.

Adam returned his attention to the matter at hand, which was driving his fiancee' home, safely.

Glancing at a roadside sign, Adam realized that they were only a mile from their destination.

Denise rose from her sleep, as her favorite song by Ray Boltz, called, "Thank You," started to play.

Together, Adam and Denise sang along with the refrain, "Thank you, for giving to the Lord. Mine was the life that was changed."

As Adam and Denise sang, joyfully, a set of headlights appeared up ahead. Adam suddenly stopped singing, but Denise continued. Adam's heart began to race, for it appeared that the headlights, that were headed straight for them, belonged to a car that was traveling in their lane.

Adam blew his horn as a warning, which alerted Denise to the oncoming car. Denise braced herself in her seat, as she watched the oncoming car in horror.

Adam decided, at the last minute, that the car was simply not going to get over into it's proper lane, so he carefully maneuvered his car into the passing lane. To his utter horror, the driver of the oncoming car decided to correct it's position, simultaneously.

Adam panicked, at the thought of the imminent collision. He completely became unnerved, lost control of his steering and smacked his small compact car, head on, into a huge oak tree. The final thought that ran through Adam's mind, directly before the collision occurred, was the familiarity of the other car and of it's driver.

Valerie let out a loud shrill, "No!"

Chris looked over at Valerie, and asked, "What is it, Val?"

"We just lost someone we love!" She replied, weeping softly.

"Who?" Chris asked.

Valerie simply shrugged her shoulders, and said, "Whoever it was, they are with our Father, now."

Chris' eyes began to tear up, as he drove on through the night.

Scott reached his destination, and parked in front of a food market. Before he shut off his headlights, he spotted Shaun standing on a street corner. The boy was leaning against a light pole, smoking a cigarette.

Scott turned off his headlights and waited inside of his car, trying to decide what to do.

Moments passed by, when all of a sudden, the boy made his way over to Scott's car.

The boy stuck his blonde head into the car and without realizing that it was Scott, he asked, "Do you want to party?"

Scott got out of his car and started to walk over to the side where the boy was standing.

Upon realizing Scott's identity, Shaun began to back away, as he said, "Oh, Man! Not you! What do you want with me, Man?"

Scott stretched out his hand and said, "I want to help you, Shaun."

"No, Man!" Shaun cried. "I don't want your help! Get away from me!"

Scott tried, in vain, to explain, "I want to help you get out of this life before it's too late."

"Too late?" The boy cried out. "Too late for who? It's already too late for you, Man. You've completely lost it."

"No I haven't," Scott cried, as he attempted to reach out to the boy.

"Get out of here, Man! You're scaring away my customers."

Scott's eyes filled with tears, so badly, that his entire face was getting soaked.

"You don't know what you're doing, Son," Scott cried.

"No!" Shaun screamed. "You're wrong! I know exactly what I'm doing. So, get out of here!"

Scott watched, helplessly, as the boy ran down the street, toward a silver station wagon that had just pulled up. Scott watched as Shaun talked to the driver, and then, as he climbed into the back seat.

Scott wiped the tears from his face, as the station wagon disappeared around a corner.

Samantha pulled up into her mother's driveway. She immediately noticed that something was wrong, because her mother's house had no lights on, whatsoever.

Slowly, climbing out of her car, Samantha made her way up to the front door. She decided to use her own key to open the door. Once inside, she fumbled for the light switch.

As soon as the lights came on, Samantha became startled by her mother's voice, as she sharply, said, "Leave them off, Samantha!"

Instead of obeying her mother's command, which was her usual style, Samantha stepped over to her mother's side.

"Why are you here lying on the couch, in the dark, Mom?" Samantha asked.

Reluctantly, Helen turned around to face her daughter.

Samantha gasped, as she looked at her mother's appearance, for she had a fat, bloody lip, a bruise on her cheek and a black eye. Samantha's heart ached for her mother, whom she loved dearly, despite everything that had ever happened during her childhood.

"What happened, Mom?"

Helen began to cry, hysterically, "It was Derek, again. He couldn't find his syringes. He became desperate.......and hostile. He just went crazy. He started calling me every name in the book. First, he tore the house apart looking for his syringes, and then, when he couldn't find them, he started going off on me."

"Mom, you've got to call the police. You need to get a restraining order against him.

You can't go on like this. Next time, he may very well kill you."

"I can't go to the police, Honey. I love the man. I just wish he would leave the drugs alone. He really is a sweet man."

Samantha told her mother that she was going into the kitchen to get something to put on her, to stop the swelling. The older woman nodded in appreciation as she laid back down to rest her eyes.

While Samantha was in the kitchen, a loud crash alerted her. She ran back into the living room to find three men standing over the couch where her mother lie, helplessly.

Chris dropped Valerie off at her apartment, and watched as she entered her building, safely, and then he drove back to the highway, where he decided to head for his favorite place to eat. He arrived at his destination, about twenty minutes later. He found a former drinking buddy sitting on a curb in front of the restaurant.

The young man had his head hanging down, and it appeared that he had been attempting to vomit.

"Hey, Lucas!" Chris called out, as he got out of his car. "Are you gonna make it?"

Lucas looked up, and despite his slightly blurred vision, he recognized Chris.

"Sure!" Lucas replied. "I'm a survivor. Don't you remember?"

"Sure I do, Man," Chris smiled. "Hey, come on in and I'll buy you a cup of coffee. What do you say?"

Lucas made a face, as if Chris had just suggested that he drink a cup of castor oil. He asked with disgust, "Coffee? Are you trying to kill me?"

Chris laughed and said, as he tried to bring his friend to his feet, "No, I'm not trying to kill you. I'm trying to sober you up, a little bit, my friend."

"Friend!" Lucas slurred. "Some friend you've been, lately. You never show up at the Blarney Stone anymore. Whatever happened to the good old days?"

Chris and Lucas attempted to enter the restaurant with the most dignity that they could manage, so as not to attract undo attention from the other patrons.

Once he managed to get Lucas seated in a booth, Chris sat across from him, and just smiled.

Rubbing his hands over his eyes, Lucas asked Chris, "What are you staring at, Chris?"

"I don't know, Lucas," Chris laughed. "I suppose I'm looking at myself just a couple of years ago."

"Say what?" Lucas asked as he attempted to place his head down upon the table.

"Oh, no you don't, Lucas," Chris warned his friend. "There will be none of that. You're not getting us kicked out of this place. After we have something to eat, then I'll drive you home."

"I've got my car parked down the street, Man. You don't need to take me home. I don't want to be a bother to anyone."

Chris began to look at the menu, while Lucas struggled to keep his head from hitting the table.

"Where are your keys, Lucas?" Chris asked, as he placed the menu down.

"In my jacket," Lucas answered.

"Let me see them, Lucas," Chris said, as he attempted to reach across the table to retrieve the keys.

"Stop!" Lucas ordered. "I'll get them out. Why do you want to see them?"

"Because," Chris explained, "you're not driving home. Not in your condition."

"Condition?" Lucas was beginning to sound boisterous. "What condition?"

"Lucas, you're smashed."

Lucas suddenly felt like the four walls of the restaurant were going to close in on him, as he began to squirm in his seat, and look around the room, nervously.

"How......how do you get off calling me a drunk, Chris? Come down off your high horse, Man. You know what it's like. There was a time when you could out drink anyone. Where do you get off, Man?"

Chris noticed that the other patrons were starting to watch them with a great deal of annoyance, as was the waitress behind the cash register.

"Just give me your keys, Lucas," Chris urged. "No one is calling you a drunk. You just over indulged a little bit, that's all. Now give me your keys before you kill yourself or, worse yet, before you kill some innocent people."

Finally, Lucas surrendered his keys over to Chris, who placed them, securely, into his own jacket pocket.

Lincoln walked a ways toward the direction of the voice which had been instrumental in chasing away the drunken thugs. He wanted to thank the person. It seemed strange, to Lincoln, but he had been unable to determine whether the voice had been that of a man or a woman.

All that he could figure out was that the voice carried with it an air of intense superiority.

Lincoln found it stranger, yet, when he discovered that there were no footprints in the sand where the voice had originated from.

A cold chill ran down his spine, as he decided to give up his search. He, then, decided that he had better head for home. As he started up the stairs, he found something lying down on the second flight of stairs.

As he knelt down to pick it up, Lincoln felt another cold chill. He grasped the object between his fingers. Instantly, he felt this ice cold chill envelop his entire body, almost, temporarily paralyzing him.

Holding the object up toward the light which was emanating from a nearby pole, he realized what he was holding, was a small locket. Opening it up, he found a photo of Adam.

Beside the photograph, on the other side of the locket, was a small inscription.

Lincoln read the small print, aloud, "To Denise. May Almighty God bless you today and always."

"That's weird!" Lincoln whispered. "Denise must have somehow dropped this. I'll have to give it to her at church."

Lincoln placed the locket deep inside of his jacket pocket as he made his way toward his car.

As the car in which Adam and Denise had been riding sat quietly and firmly against a tree, the driver of the other car came over to investigate.

Denise began to murmur, unintelligibly. Blood was pouring from her forehead. Glass lay strewn everywhere.

The other driver peered in at the couple, and noticed that Adam was either dead or unconscious.

As Denise struggled to open her blood soaked eyes, the driver panicked and returned to their car, rapidly.

Denise managed to open one eye, as the station wagon made it's swift getaway.

A sharp pain ran through her body, as she glanced skyward. It seemed, to her, that the night sky was suddenly illuminated by something. White clouds, along with two outstretched hands appeared, beckoning her to come. They seemed to be beckoning her to come to a place where there would be no more pain, no more sorrow.

Seconds later, Denise breathed her last, as she joined her fiancee', Adam, in the almighty hereafter.

Samantha demanded to know what was going on, as she ran into her mother's living room.

First, she noticed the men standing over her mother, and then she noticed, that they had gained entrance into the house, by forcing the door in.

"Who are you? What do you want?" Samantha bravely demanded.

"We're the three stooges, Lady," one man said, with a toothless grin. "We've come to pillage and plunder."

"You'd better leave, or I'll have to call the police," Samantha warned, desperately trying to disguise her natural fear.

"Police!" The man exclaimed. "And why would you want to do such a thing?"

"What do you want with my mother?" Samantha asked.

"It's not your mother we have a score to settle with, Sister," the man explained, as he sauntered over toward Samantha. "It's your low down scummy, dirt bag of a step-father we have a beef with. You see, he owes us a great deal of money."

"So," Samantha's voice was taking on a slight quiver, "is this your usual way of making collections? I mean, do you always go around ripping people's doors off of their hinges?"

The trio of men grinned maliciously, and their spokesman replied, "Yeah, do you got a problem with that, Sister?"

Samantha went over to her mother and asked her, "What's going on here, Mama? Where's Derek?"

Helen's eyes suddenly filled with terror as she quickly shook her head no.

"Come on, Mama," the man pleaded, in a mocking tone. "Where's Derek?"

Again, the older woman shook her head, defiantly.

Finally, the intruder, upon growing very impatient, decided to speed up the interrogation process, by grabbing Samantha by the hair, jerking her backward, away from the couch.

"Come on, now, Mama. Tell us where your hubby is, before we hurt your beautiful daughter, here, twice as bad as Derek obviously, did you."

Helen struggled to sit up on the couch as she watched her daughter attempt to free herself of the intruder.

"Please," she begged. "Don't hurt my daughter. Derek is working at the bar, tonight. Leave us alone."

"What bar?" The man demanded, as he tightened his grip upon Samantha's hair.

"The Eagle's Eye!"

"Thank you, very much!" He replied, sarcastically, as he flung Samantha down on the couch beside her mother.

After the men departed, Samantha cried, "Mama, come home with me for awhile. It isn't safe for you here"

Helen didn't need time to consider her daughter's suggestion, as she struggled to rise from the couch.

The following morning found Valerie waking up at the crack of dawn. As she prepared her breakfast, the telephone rang.

Placing her toast and jelly down, Valerie answered the telephone and heard a familiar voice on the other end.

"Well, hello Pastor Mark!" Valerie said cheerfully. "What's up?"

The young preacher's voice took on a serious tone, as he explained, "My wife didn't come home last night, Valerie. Did she, by any chance, come by your place?"

Valerie placed the phone against her other ear, and answered, "No, she didn't. Do you think something has happened to her?"

"I pray to God that she simply went to visit someone, lost track of the time, and then decided to spend the night."

"Wouldn't she have called you, if that were the case?"

Pastor Mark replied sorrowfully, "No, she wouldn't have, Valerie. You see, we had a terrible fight, yesterday, and she stormed out of here in a cloud of dust."

Valerie remembered the premonition that had plagued her last night. She didn't wish to add to her pastor's concern, by telling him about it. So, she decided not to mention it, at all.

"Oh," Pastor Mark remembered the other reason for his call, "by the way, did you hear about Adam and Denise?"

Valerie asked, "Do you mean about their tying the knot sooner than expected?"

Pastor Mark cried slightly, "No! I mean about their accident."

"Accident?" Valerie cried out. "Denise and Adam were in an accident?"

"Yes, Valerie," Pastor Mark reported solemnly. "I'm afraid Adam's car struck a tree, head on, last night."

Valerie felt her chest tightening, as she realized that another one of her premonitions was mysteriously, coming true.

"How did it happen? Are they all right?" Valerie asked, even though she was quite certain that she already knew the answer.

Pastor Mark replied softly, "Adam was killed instantly. Denise followed suit, a short time later. I'm afraid that we've lost them both. They're with our Lord in Heaven, now."

Valerie stared into space, as if she were in a trance.

Scott spent several hours cruising the streets, hoping to spot the car that had whisked Shaun away into the night. He was extremely concerned about the boy's welfare. There was no telling what kind of danger the young boy was getting himself into.

Scott had, finally, abandoned his search around two in the morning, and decided that the boy was wiry enough to get himself out of any tight spots, so he called it a night.

He hoped that the boy still held on to his business card, but he felt positive that Shaun, most likely, had discarded it, somewhere.

When Scott awoke that morning, he noticed that there was a message on his answering machine. Playing the message back, Scott was relieved to hear the young boy's voice.

The recording said, "Hey, Man! I'm sorry, Man! You were right! These guys are real scum! I...I....I'm not feeling too well, Man! This guy......this guy......he.....help me, Man! I'm at East 20th and Lakeside."

Scott quickly dressed, noticing that the time of the call was only ten minutes ago.

Darting outside at lightning speed, Scott ran to his car, and peeled out of his parking space, attracting the attention of an elderly woman who was walking her dog.

As Scott sped down Lakeside, he estimated that it would only take him about fifteen minutes to reach the spot that Shaun had called him from.

Upon reaching the intersection of 20th and Lakeside, Scott jumped out of his car and immediately, began to look around. He spotted the telephone booth, that the boy must have used. But, the boy was not in sight so Scott said a quick, silent prayer, that he would turn out to be, relatively, unharmed.

Moments later, Scott heard a soft groaning coming from behind a garbage dumpster.

Carefully stepping around fallen debris and broken glass, Scott maneuvered his way to the rear of the dumpster, where he found a semi-conscious Shaun lying in a corner in a pool of blood.

"Shaun!" Scott called out. "What did that guy do to you?"

Shaun cried into Scott's arms, "He attacked me with a butcher knife. He said he hated my kind and that he was going to kill us all, one by one."

"How did you get away from him?" Scott asked, while trying to get the boy to his feet.

"I kicked him in the groin. He dropped the knife, and then the phone rang. I made my way out of there while he was distracted."

Scott observed the cut on Shaun's forearm, and said, "I've got to get you to a hospital, Shaun."

Suddenly, the boy began to resist Scott's aid, as he shouted, "No! You can't take me to a hospital. They'll call my mother. And then I'll have to go back home. You don't know what her boyfriend will do to me."

Scott felt more pity for Shaun, than he had ever felt, before. The boy had the roughest life imaginable. Scott decided to take the boy in, and to call Valerie over with some bandages and medicine.

Lincoln awoke that morning with the urgent desire to return the lost locket to Denise. He decided that he would pay Pastor Mark a visit, for he recalled that his pastor was scheduled to see Denise and Adam that morning.

Getting dressed quickly, Lincoln bounded out of the door, and headed straight for his car. As the engine turned over, Lincoln automatically turned on his radio.

The local news came on, and Lincoln listened as the female reporter performed her job.

Lincoln heard the woman say, "A local couple was pronounced dead on arrival at St. John General Hospital, late last night. It appears that their automobile collided head on with a tree, along Lake Road. Their identities are being withheld until family members can be notified. The accident is still under investigation."

Lincoln changed the station to another one that played soft, instrumental music. Suddenly, Lincoln recalled Valerie's prediction, that there was going to be an accident last night. So, he changed his course and headed straight for Valerie's apartment.

Lincoln arrived at the Rose Meadows Apartment complex in a few short minutes. He noticed that Valerie's car was not in the parking lot, but then he remembered that Chris had driven her home, last night.

Lincoln ran up to the front door of the building and rang Valerie's apartment number.

Soon, Valerie's voice came over the intercom, sounding a bit distressed.

"Val, it's me, Lincoln. Is this a bad time?"

The sound of the buzzer filled the air, indicating to Lincoln that he had been granted entrance.

Passing by two elderly women, Lincoln greeted them cheerfully.

The women responded with suspicious glances, as they turned and watched him climb the stairs, taking two steps at a time.

Lincoln heard one of the women say to the other, "What's he doing here?"

As he rounded a turn in the stairs, he heard the other woman respond, "He's probably up to no good."

Lincoln suppressed his anger long enough to reach Valerie's door, on the second floor.

When she finally opened the door to allow Lincoln to enter, he found that her eyes were damp.

"What's wrong, Val?" Lincoln asked.

Valerie gave Lincoln a hug, and cried, "Another one of my predictions came true."

Lincoln, while still hugging Valerie, asked, "Was it the couple on the news? They wouldn't release their identities. Were they people from the church?"

Valerie whispered, "Yes," while tears flowed down her cheeks, again.

"It was Adam and Denise!" Valerie managed to say, in between sobs.

Lincoln released his embrace, reached inside his pocket and brought out the locket.

"What's that?" Valerie asked, as she wiped the tears from her face.

"I found this last night, after all of you left," Lincoln explained.

Valerie took the locket in her trembling hands, turned it over and over, and then she opened it, while Lincoln watched.

Valerie let out a gasp of surprise, as she gazed at the picture of Adam.

"It's kind of ironic, isn't it, Val?" Lincoln asked, while Valerie read the inscription, silently.

"How so, Lincoln?" Valerie asked.

"It's just strange that I would discover this locket lying on the stairs at the beach, at precisely the same time that they were involved in their accident."

"Who do you suppose we should give it to?" Valerie asked.

"I think that we ought to give it to Pastor Mark, and let him decide what to do with it."

Valerie concurred. She was about to get Lincoln a glass of tea, when the telephone rang.

Valerie answered it, immediately, and heard Scott's voice on the other end.

"Val," Scott's voice sounded extremely agitated. "I need you to bring your first aid kit over here, to my place right away."

Valerie glanced over toward Lincoln, and said, "I don't have my car, Scott. Chris brought me home, last night."

Lincoln intervened, "I'll take you wherever you need to go, Val."

"Never mind, Scott," Val smiled. "Lincoln's here. He's offered me a lift. By the way, what's wrong?"

"I'll explain everything when you get here. Please hurry."

After Valerie and Scott ended their conversation, Valerie went in search of her first aid kit.

Samantha awoke to the smell of coffee brewing. She rubbed the sleep from her eyes, as she made her way downstairs. Upon finding her mother washing a few of her late night dishes, Samantha rushed over to her mother and said, "Mama, you're still very weak. You shouldn't be standing on your feet."

Helen smiled, as she said, "I want to be useful."

Samantha said, "You'll be much more useful, Mama, if you just relax and take care of yourself. Now, go and sit down, somewhere. I'll fix us some breakfast."

Helen sat down in the living room and picked up the local morning paper. The headlines were of no particular interest to her, however, the story at the bottom of the page caught her eye.

"Look at this, Dear," Helen called out to her daughter.

As Samantha entered the room, she found her mother referring to a newspaper article.

"It says that there was a fatal car accident, last night out on Lake Road, near the beach. Wasn't that where you and your friends were yesterday?"

Samantha asked, while nervously wringing her hands inside of a dish towel, "Does it say who died in that accident, Mama?"

"No," she replied. "They won't be releasing that information until relatives are notified."

Pastor Mark paced around his kitchen floor, nervously, checking his wristwatch every few minutes.

Finally, he decided to telephone another one of his parishioners.

After dialing the phone, the preacher heard Samantha's voice on the other end.

"I'm sorry for calling you so early, Samantha," Pastor Mark began. "But I was wondering if you have seen or heard from Maggie, lately."

"No, I haven't, Pastor Mark. Is something wrong?"

Pastor Mark replied, "I certainly hope not. You see, she never came home last night. She said she was going for a drive."

"I'm sure she's fine, Pastor Mark," Samantha said, trying to sound reassuring.

"By the way," Mark continued, "have you heard, by now, about the terrible accident out on Lake Road, last night?"

"Yes," Samantha confirmed, as she added, "my mother was just reading the newspaper article to me. Was it anyone we know?"

Like Valerie, somehow, Samantha also felt she already knew the answer to this question.

"Yes! I'm afraid it was Adam and Denise!"

Samantha dropped the phone, and totally lost her equilibrium.

"Hello? Samantha, are you still there?"

Samantha's mother took the phone in her hand and informed the preacher that Samantha had suddenly taken ill, from the shock.

After hanging up the receiver, Pastor Mark heard the front door to his small frame house, close.

As he rounded the corner, and entered the small living room, he found his wife seated on the sofa. She looked as if she hadn't slept all night long.

"Maggie!" He exclaimed. "Where have you been? I've been worried sick. I've been calling all over town, trying to locate you."

Maggie raised up her heavy eyelids, and glared at her husband, demanding, "You've what?"

Pastor Mark repeated, "I've been calling some of our friends, trying to locate you."

Maggie's voice took on a strange, seriously bitter tone, of which Mark was not accustomed to. Mark winced, as he heard his wife say, "So, what you're trying to tell me, is that the entire congregation of the Church of Faith in Christ, knows that the young respectable Pastor Mark has a wife who doesn't come home at night. Thanks a lot, Mark. You are sure some piece of art."

Mark attempted to reason with his young wife of only two years, by explaining, "I was worried about you."

"Well," Maggie curled up in the sofa, yawned lazily, and said, "Markie, my pet, you need not worry about me. I can take care of myself."

Mark watched, helplessly, as Maggie drifted off to sleep, without removing her jacket or her shoes.

CHAPTER TWO

PRAYERS

Scott let Lincoln and Valerie in. He, then, led them into his spare bedroom, where they found Shaun lying on a bed, curled up in a fetal position.

Valerie asked, "What on earth happened to him?"

Scott, nervously, ran his fingers through his hair, as he tried to explain, "Shaun is a street kid, and he kind of got roughed up a bit."

"I'd say!" Lincoln commented, with a whistle.

Valerie instructed Scott and Lincoln to wait outside of the room while she examined the boy's wounds.

While out in the hallway, Lincoln informed Scott about Adam and Denise.

Scott remarked, "I guess there is some validity to Val's predictions."

Lincoln rubbed his hand over his face and commented, "They were about to spend the rest of their lives together."

Scott attempted to look on the bright side of the tragic incident, as he said, "I guess, now, they'll be spending eternity, together."

Lincoln managed a smile, and nodded his head.

Moments later, Valerie emerged from the room, and told Scott, "He has a cut on his forearm. It should heal in a week or so. He seems terribly distraught over this whole ordeal. Do you have any idea how it happened, Scott?"

Scott shrugged his shoulders, and said, "The kid didn't tell me much. I think it was a matter of being in the wrong place at the wrong time."

Valerie wrote something on a slip of paper, and told Scott, "You can get this over the counter, Scott. It should calm him down a bit. Just follow the directions on the bottle. He should start to improve in a day or so. I'm going back in there to dress the wound. You could pour us a couple cups of coffee, Scott."

Scott quickly obliged the nurse and headed straight for his kitchen, followed closely behind by Lincoln.

Like clockwork, Chris ate lunch, everyday, at the same diner. It was convenient, because it was right next door to the factory, where he was employed, as an arc welder.

Chris usually ate his lunch with a few co-workers. Today, however, he had arranged for Lucas to meet him there.

Nervously, Chris looked at his watch and noticed that Lucas was now ten minutes late.

Chris began to doubt whether his former drinking buddy was even going to show up.

All of a sudden, Lucas came walking through the door. He was followed in by a young woman with blonde hair.

Chris swallowed a bite of his sandwich, and then held out his hand to Lucas and his companion.

Lucas shook Chris' hand, uncertainly. He, then, introduced the young woman, "This here's Julia, Chris. We're kind of going steady."

Chris shook Julia's hand and then urged them to be seated.

"Why all of the urgency, Chris?" Lucas asked, as he and Julia got themselves settled in their seats.

"I wanted to tell you why I haven't been showing up at the Blarney Stone these past two years," Chris explained, while trying to include Julia in the conversation, although he hadn't expected Lucas to bring anyone with him.

Lucas laughed and asked, sarcastically, "What happened, Chris? Did you find religion or something?"

Chris smiled, as he said, "Or something!"

"What's that, there?" Lucas asked, as he pointed to a book that Chris had his right hand on.

Chris held up the book, and replied, proudly, "This is the Word of God!"

Lucas laughed, a little uneasily, "Oh, for a minute there, I thought it might a Bible or something."

Chris laughed and pretended to knock Lucas in the head with a spoon, as he said, "It is a Bible, you Knucklehead!"

The ice was now broken, and Chris felt that this would be the perfect time to introduce the gospel to his friend.

Scott called his boss, and said that there was an emergency that he had to take care of. He told him that he would be unable to make it in to work, today.

Fortunately, Scott had a very understanding boss, who was, also, a born again Christian.

Scott checked on Shaun after Lincoln and Valerie left. The boy was resting comfortably, thanks to the medicine that Lincoln had been kind enough to go after.

A memory suddenly returned to Scott, as he watched Shaun sleeping. It was not a welcomed memory, however. Scott's hands began to tremble, uncontrollably, as he fought to erase this memory from his mind.

Scott was remembering when he was around Shaun's age, and he was spending a night out with one of his own mother's many boyfriends. The man, slowly, got him drunk that night, without his becoming aware of it.

Scott remembered passing out in the back of some liquor store. The last thing he had recalled, that night, was his mother's latest boyfriend staring at him, with an empty bottle in one hand and a gun in the other.

When Scott had come to, he had awakened in the back seat of an old car. The smell of liquor pervaded the car. Scott remembered that he had wanted to vomit.

The next thing he recalled was discovering that he had been stripped of his clothes, and a young girl was asleep in the front seat, also minus clothes.

Scott recalled the incredible sense of having his privacy completely violated for the very first time. He recalled the embarrassment that he and that young girl felt, when they realized the predicament that had placed them both in an extremely compromising position.

As Scott watched Shaun sleep, he wondered just how much the boy had experienced, already, in the short time that he had been living on the streets. Scott recalled every dirty old man that he had ever encountered during his own time spent out there. These horrifying memories that, occasionally, haunted him, made Scott, immediately get down on his knees and begin to pray to the Lord, with the utmost urgency.

Shaun, suddenly, awoke and rubbed his eyes, as he struggled to focus upon Scott.

"What are you doing, Scott?" Shaun asked.

Scott finished praying, and walked over to Shaun and answered, "I was praying for you."

Shaun grinned, and said, "Wow! That's really nice. No one has ever prayed for me before."

Pastor Mark got up from his desk and went over to the door. Upon opening it, he found two of his parishioners. They both looked a bit shaken.

"Valerie! Lincoln! Come on in," he said, as he stepped aside.

Valerie unzipped her jacket, as she said, "Lincoln found this last night."

Lincoln handed the locket to the preacher, and then he turned to find Maggie stirring around on the sofa.

"Hello, Mrs. Jenner!" Lincoln greeted.

Valerie apologized, "I hope we aren't disturbing you, Maggie."

Maggie became fully awake when she realized that they had unexpected company. She sat straight up and pulled her jacket down for it had bunched up as she slept.

"It's quite all right, Valerie," Maggie assured her guests, after shooting her husband an angry glare for not rousing her before he answered the door.

Pastor Mark opened the locket, and after realizing who it belonged to, he gasped, "My good Lord! This belongs to Denise! Where did you find this, Lincoln?"

Lincoln explained how he found the locket at the beach, and then Maggie interrupted, "What's the big deal? We'll just return it to Denise, today, when she and Adam come over for their appointment."

"We can't do that, Maggie," Mark informed his wife.

"Why not?" Maggie asked, as she struggled to stand up. "Did they cancel the wedding?"

Mark shot Valerie and Lincoln a concerned glance, as he watched his wife struggle to maintain her balance.

"Adam and Denise were killed last night, Maggie," Valerie explained.

Maggie fell back onto the sofa and asked, "Why? How?"

Lincoln explained, "They were killed shortly after leaving the Bible study, last night. Their car was found along Lake Road. They had apparently collided with a huge old oak tree, somehow."

Maggie's eyes immediately began to fill with tears.

Chris glanced at his wristwatch and realized that he did not have time to explain everything, properly, to Lucas, so he was forced to apologize, as he prepared to go back to work.

"You're both invited to the Church of Faith in Christ, this Sunday. There's going to be a special singer. I know that both of you will really enjoy it. I've got to get back to work. I'm sorry! Lucas, call me."

After Chris left, Lucas thumbed through the few small tracts that Chris had left for him to read. One said, "Are you saved? If you were to die today, where would you go? Heaven or Hell?"

Another one said, "Jesus Christ died on the cross to save us all from sin."

Lucas turned toward his girlfriend and grinned, as he said, "My best friend has turned into a Jesus freak."

Julia took one of the tracts and began to read it, silently.

As Samantha, finally, got over the shock, she sat up and looked around the room. She spotted her mother dialing the telephone.

"Who are you calling, Mama?" Samantha asked.

"Derek," Helen answered, while still dialing. "I have to see if he's all right."

"No, Mama!" Samantha shouted. She quickly jumped up from her chair, and bounded over to the telephone. She added, "If Derek doesn't kill you first, his hoodlum friends will."

"He's still my husband, Samantha Rose!"

Samantha, gently, placed the receiver down and helped her mother over to the couch, as she said, "Mama, you've got to get that man out of your life. He's dangerous."

"But, I still love him!"

"Well," Samantha warned, "this love you feel for Derek, may very well become fatal. I worry about you."

Helen grinned, as she suggested, "Why don't you just pray to that God of yours?"

"Touche'!" Samantha laughed. "As usual, you always know what to say."

Samantha prepared herself for some silent prayer, while her mother looked on, approvingly.

Later that evening, after her shift at the hospital was over, Valerie decided to pop in on Scott, to see how he and Shaun were getting on.

She felt this strange sense of foreboding, as she knocked at Scott's door. Her fears were realized, for the look on Scott's face affirmed her preconception.

"What's wrong, Scott?" Valerie asked. "Has Shaun taken a turn for the worse?"

Scott ushered Valerie inside, and as she removed her jacket, he explained, "Earlier, I was praying for Shaun. He awoke and saw me doing this. At first, he was glad. But, then, about an hour later, he took on this completely different attitude. It's as if he's got some kind of split personality, or something. He, suddenly, turned into this incredibly rude, insensitive little kid."

Valerie tossed her jacket over a nearby chair, walked into the living room and asked, "Well, where is he? I'll speak to him. Perhaps you're too emotionally involved with the situation."

Scott explained, while nervously running his hands through his hair, "He split!"

"Where did he go? I thought that he was scared to death to go back home."

31

Scott flopped down onto the sofa and took in a deep breath, slowly released it, and then he shrugged his shoulders, and said, "I haven't the foggiest idea."

Valerie, immediately, dropped down to her knees, and prayed aloud, "Dear Lord, I come to you precious Jesus, to humbly ask for your help. I come to you out of concern for Shaun. He's a very troubled young boy. He doesn't know you yet, Lord. But I know you are watching over him, Lord. I pray that you help Scott, here, find the right words that will help change this young boy's life. I pray that Shaun will find his way to you, Lord, before it's too late for him. He is living out a very dangerous lifestyle. He's too afraid to go home, and it seems that he is trying to find a place where he belongs. He belongs in your precious fold, Lord. Guide him through this rough time. Guide him home, Lord. We praise your name, Lord! We thank you, Lord!"

Scott opened his eyes, smiled over at Valerie, and said, "Amen!"

Pastor Mark and Lincoln paid Peggy Washington a visit that evening. They were delighted to discover that Rosemary Harrison was also present.

After Peggy gathered their jackets, she invited everyone into the living room, where they made themselves comfortable.

Pastor Mark noticed, immediately, Rosemary's bloodshot eyes, as he began to console the two grieving mothers.

"I'm so sorry, ladies, for your losses. If it's any comfort, Rosemary, I heard that Adam didn't suffer. He was taken from us, almost immediately, following this unfortunate accident."

Rosemary hugged Pastor Mark, as she cried, "Adam and Denise were to be married next month."

Peggy's eyes began to get watery, as she listened to her good friend weep.

Lincoln opened up his closed fist and stepped over toward Rosemary, who turned to him and asked, "What's this, Lincoln?"

Lincoln replied, "I found this at the beach, yesterday, following our Bible study."

Rosemary took the item from Lincoln and then, she asked, "Who does it belong to?"

Lincoln instructed her, "Open it up. It's a locket."

Peggy watched, silently, as Rosemary opened the locket.

Rosemary gasped, "It's a picture of my Adam. I don't understand."

Peggy caught a glimpse of the locket, nodded her head, and told her friend, "Rosemary, read what's written on the other side."

Peggy's tears began to flow, as Rosemary read aloud, "To Denise. May Almighty God bless you today and always."

"Denise must have dropped it somehow," Pastor Mark suggested, politely.

Rosemary turned toward Peggy and the two women fell into each others arms, crying softly.

Pastor Mark and Lincoln bowed their heads. Pastor Mark began to pray, "Dear Lord, hear our prayer. I come to you, Lord, with a heavy heart. We ask you Lord, to help our sisters in Christ, Rosemary and Peggy, during their time of grief. We ask you Lord to help them and to guide them. Show them your incredible mercy, Lord. They both loved their children, Lord. Adam and Denise will be sorely missed. They, as you know, were to be joined in holy matrimony, Lord. They were about to spend the rest of their lives, serving you, Lord, together. We just ask you to comfort these grieving mothers, and to strengthen them. Show them that they can get through this, Lord, forever praising your name. Guide them, Oh Lord, along the paths of righteousness. Help them in case they should falter along the way. Let them be shining examples of the loving children of you, our Heavenly Father. In the name of our Lord Jesus Christ, we pray. Amen."

Chris stayed up later than usual, that night, for he had been attempting to get caught up on his reading. As he opened his Bible up to the Book of Psalms, he read aloud, "Psalm One. The Way of the Righteous and the End of the Ungodly. Blessed is the man who walks not in the counsel of the ungodly, Nor stands in the path of sinners, Nor sits in the seat of the scornful; But his delight is in the law of the Lord, And in his law he meditates day and night."

Suddenly, Chris' phone rang. Reaching out and picking up the cordless telephone receiver, which sat on a night stand beside his bed, Chris said, "Hello."

The voice on the other end was, at first, unrecognizable, to Chris, but after a moment passed by, he realized that the caller was Lucas' girlfriend, Julia.

"Chris, I really would like to talk to you again, if it's ever possible," Julia said, nervously.

"Julia?" Chris asked, "Where's Lucas?"

Julia's voice took on a strange tone, as she explained, "He went out with some guys. I think they've gone to shoot some pool, or something."

"Why didn't you join them, Julia? Are you feeling sick?" Chris asked out of concern.

"No!" Julia replied. "I just can't live that lifestyle, anymore. It's really taking it's toll on me."

"Julia," Chris smiled, "did you by any chance read those tracts that I left on the table at the restaurant, earlier today?"

Julia confirmed Chris' assumption.

"Good girl!" Chris encouraged the young girl. "My invitation to church still stands, if you and Lucas would like to join me."

"Well," Julia began slowly, "I can't speak for Lucas, but I would like to come to church, tomorrow."

Chris suddenly began to beam with delight, as he almost shouted, "Excellent! Give me your address and I'll pick you up, in the morning."

Scott and Valerie decided to return to the place where Shaun usually hung around. The night air had begun to grow rather crisp, by the time they reached their destination.

Scott got out of the car first. He glanced around the deserted street and he began to feel a little apprehensive.

Valerie, slowly, emerged from Scott's car, and she, too, looked a bit distressed.

"Why don't we split up, Scott? I'll go off in this direction, and you head off that way. Maybe one of us will run into him."

Scott, reluctantly, agreed to Valerie's suggestion, as they started walking off in their respective directions.

Valerie wrapped her sweater around herself tighter, for she could feel the breeze from the nearby lake begin to increase it's velocity.

Nearby, Autumn leaves were swirling about in a circle. A black cat with emerald eyes slithered by Valerie as she neared a corner. Instinctively, Valerie took a left turn. A few feet ahead, she saw a shadowy figure leaning against a brick building.

"Hello!" Valerie called out.

Meanwhile, Scott had also made a turn down a side street. He saw, up ahead, a gang of young men standing in a circle. They seemed to be passing something around to one another. Scott supposed it to be a joint or something.

The men turned to face Scott as he drew nearer.

Scott sensed that they deemed him as unwelcome, which made him feel a little uncomfortable.

One of the gang members stepped over toward Scott, got directly in his face and asked, "What do you want, Gringo?"

Scott stood his ground and desperately tried to disguise his nervousness. He replied, "I'm looking for a little blonde kid."

The gang member grinned, as he looked around at the others guys. Laughing, he informed them, "Gringo, here, wants to score tonight with a little blonde boy."

Scott's cheeks began to turn bright red with embarrassment, as the entire gang laughed.

During the laughter, Scott noticed a figure hiding in the shadows. The figure was shivering in the cold and appeared to be wincing in pain.

Quickly, Scott rushed over to the cowering figure, and discovered it to be Shaun.

"Shaun!" Scott cried out. "What happened to you?"

The next thing that Scott felt, was a vicious blow to the back of his head, which sent him sprawling down to the hard concrete below.

Pastor Mark returned home that night, after making a few rounds of visiting his parishioners, to find an incredibly strong aroma, coming from the kitchen. He placed his coat on a nearby chair, and then, made his way into the kitchen, where he found his wife seated at the table.

Maggie was lazily thumbing through a magazine, while Peggy Washington stood with her back toward him, stirring a pot.

"Peggy!" Pastor Mark exclaimed. "What, on earth, are you doing here?"

Peggy turned toward Pastor Mark, smiled, and replied, "Maggie called me up and asked me for my recipe for beef stew. It sounded a bit too complicated for her, so I decided to come over here and lend her a hand."

Maggie looked up from her magazine and caught the look of bewilderment in her husband's eyes.

"Maggie!" Pastor Mark exclaimed. "How could you bother Peggy at a time like this?"

Peggy rushed to Maggie's defense, as she quickly explained, "Oh, Mark, it's no bother at all. Really!"

Pastor Mark watched, helplessly, as Peggy continued to stir the simmering vegetables and beef, while his wife continued to flip through the pages of a magazine.

Peggy noticed the growing tension, so she turned toward Maggie, and said, "All you need to do, now, Maggie, is stir the vegetables and meat every once in awhile. It should simmer for about fifteen minutes more. I should be getting home, now."

Maggie stood up, gave Peggy a hug, and whispered softly, "Thanks a million, Peg! I'll see you in church, tomorrow."

Pastor Mark watched as Maggie ushered Peggy to the door. After she returned to the kitchen, Maggie found her husband stirring the pot of stew.

Feeling the tension in the air, growing every second, Maggie attempted to ease things as she commented, "Well, it seems that pot isn't the only thing stewing, tonight. What's the matter with you, Mark?"

Pastor Mark placed the stirring fork down upon the stove, turned toward his wife and replied, "You're asking me what's wrong? You call one of my parishioners over here to cook us dinner and you want to know what's wrong with me? Good Lord, Maggie! Peggy Washington has just lost her daughter and you have the audacity to invite her over here to cook beef stew for us."

Maggie stormed out of the kitchen, as she shouted, "I was just trying to be a good wife to you. You're always complaining about me not measuring up to the duties of a pastor's wife. There's just no pleasing you, Mark Jenner. This meal was supposed to be a surprise."

Valerie found the shadowy figure to be that of a young woman, who was obviously, pregnant.

"Hello, there!" Valerie repeated. "I was wondering if you could help me. I'm looking for a young boy. His name is Shaun. He has wavy blonde hair. He's not very big for his fourteen years. Have you seen him around here, by any chance?"

The young woman began to rub her stomach, soothingly, as she glanced over toward Valerie, with obvious disinterest in her eyes.

"No. I haven't seen the kid," she replied, as she returned her gaze toward the building across the street.

Valerie asked, "How many months along are you?"

The girl answered, "Nine! Why do you ask?"

Valerie replied, "It's just that I'm a nurse, and I was curious. By the way, my name is Valerie. What's yours?"

The girl shook Valerie's outstretched hand, and answered, "I'm Alice!"

"Do you mind if I ask you why you're standing out here in the cold, this late at night, Alice?"

Alice shrugged her shoulders, and replied, "You can ask me anything you want to, Nurse Valerie."

As Val was about to say something else, Alice suddenly gripped the underside of her belly and groaned.

"What's wrong, Alice?" Valerie asked.

"I think it's almost time, Nurse Valerie," Alice grimaced.

"Who is your doctor, Alice?" Valerie asked, excitedly.

"He's a quack, Nurse Valerie," Alice winced in pain.

"I've got to get you to the car, Alice," Valerie said, as she began to help Alice walk along.

Samantha found herself tossing and turning that night, so she decided to check on her mother who insisted upon sleeping in the living room on the couch. As Samantha entered the living room, she found her mother sleeping peacefully. Samantha smiled contentedly.

She started for the kitchen to get something to drink, because her throat was feeling a little parched. After choosing orange juice, she brought the small cup back into the living room, where she curled up on a huge overstuffed easy chair, wrapping her long, flowing housecoat around her legs.

As she quietly sipped a her juice, an unwelcome memory returned to her, coming at her with all the vengeance of an angry lioness who had just witnessed the merciless slaughter of her cubs.

Samantha's memory flashed back to an incident from her childhood. She had only been a mere eight years old, when she crawled out of bed in the middle of the night. Unnoticed by her parents, who were presently engaged in one of their many arguments, young Samantha sat silently in the hall, just outside of the living room, where her mother was sitting on the couch and her father was standing, threateningly over his wife.

Samantha recalled the smell of beer, as her parents argued, relentlessly. The smell was so strong, that she was afraid that she might vomit from the foul odor. She hated it when her father drank, for it seemed to transform him from the loving, kind man he was normally, into some sort of irrational demon.

As Samantha peered around the corner, she discovered that her father was waving something in the air, which he held in his right hand. As she focused on the shiny object, her jaw dropped down in shock. She realized that it was a small revolver. Samantha felt puzzled for she never knew that her father even owned such a weapon.

Samantha distinctly heard her father ask her mother, "Do you dare me to pull the trigger, Helen?"

"You're intoxicated, Guy!" Helen had said, with a slight quivering voice.

Guy swallowed another mouthful of beer, and then, as Samantha watched from her hidden vantage point, she witnessed her father point the gun at his head, with a trembling hand.

Samantha remembered wanting to intervene in this scene as it was unfolding before her, but she sat unable to move, as if some force was holding her down. She attempted to make her presence known, but as she opened her mouth to speak, she discovered that she couldn't even utter a peep.

Samantha watched with wide eyes filled with horror, as her father came through with his drunken threat, as he pulled the trigger, thus sending a bullet directly into his brain.

Samantha recalled her own blood curdling scream filling the entire house, as she watched her father slump to the floor, in a pool of bright red blood.

Samantha twitched uncontrollably in the overstuffed chair and almost spilled her juice on herself, as she tried to shake this horrendous image from her mind.

She placed the cup down on a nearby coffee table. She dropped to her knees to pray. She felt the need to converse with her almighty redeemer. She needed to banish these memories that Satan was inflicting upon her.

Quietly, Samantha whispered, "Dear Lord, I am troubled by memories of the past. I need your divine intervention, to help me conquer my fears. I was merely a young girl when I witnessed this terrible incident, that took my father away from me, forever. I did so love my father when he wasn't drinking, when he wasn't trying to destroy himself and others around him. I realize, now, that my father must have been a very troubled soul. I wish that I could have been able to somehow intervene. I wish that I could have been able to say something, to remind him how much I loved and cared for him. Perhaps, I could have prevented this tragedy. I know there isn't anything I can do about it, now, Lord. I just pray, Lord, that you would send down your unlimited mercy upon me, for I am continuously feeling tormented by these memories. They are succeeding to drag down my spirits, and I wish to walk in your light. I want to help others who need you, Lord, in their lives. I can't be one of your disciples if I am troubled by my past. Please help me to be strong. Show me the way, Lord. Thank you, Lord. You are truly worthy to be praised. In the name of our Lord Jesus Christ, we pray. Amen."

Samantha smiled, as she watched her mother sleep peacefully, for the time being, at least.

Alice and Valerie reached the car. They found, to their dismay, that Scott had automatically locked the doors, before he had set out to locate Shaun.

"What's off in that direction, Alice?" Valerie asked as she pointed toward the direction that Scott had gone in.

Alice replied, nervously, "A small gang hangs out around that last building down there."

"Can you make it? My friend, Scott, went off in that direction. He can help us."

Alice nodded as she held onto her stomach. Slowly, the women made their way down the deserted street.

After they finally reached the corner of the building, Alice found the gang that she had mentioned earlier, standing around in a circle, which was their usual style.

Valerie said a quick prayer that Alice and her baby would be all right.

As the women neared the gang of young men, Alice addressed one of the members, with half a grin, "What's going on, Rico?"

Rico smiled at the sight of Alice, and laughed, "Nothing much here, my lady. But it looks to me like you are about to give way to that little bambino any time now."

"As usual, Rico," Alice grinned, "you're the clever one."

As Rico and Alice exchanged lines, Valerie glanced around for Scott.

Alice noticed the fear and anxiety that her new found friend was exhibiting, so she asked Rico, "Have you seen her friend Scott, Rico?"

Rico became nervous all of a sudden, as he began to glance around, while digging his hands deep into his pockets.

"No!" He shouted. "What makes you think I've seen anyone?"

Alice smiled at Valerie, and informed her that Rico was lying through his shiny white teeth.

Valerie asked her, "How do you know he's lying?"

Alice replied, "It's simple, Valerie. Just watch his body language. See how he fidgets and won't even look me straight in the face. He's lying through his teeth, I tell you."

Valerie began to look around and then she let out a gasp, when she discovered Scott lying on the ground, semi-conscious, beside Shaun, who was also in some sort of pain.

"Scott!" Valerie shouted. "Can you hear me?"

Scott stirred slightly at the sound of Valerie's voice. He murmured, "Thank God!"

Alice turned a disappointed face toward Rico and asked him, "Rico, did you do this to Scott?"

Rico avoided Alice's stern glare, by looking off into another direction.

Valerie directed her next question toward Rico and asked, "And what's happened to Shaun?"

Alice answered, "He was probably injected with heroin or something, Val. There's a rival gang who has this sick ritual of injecting young children with that junk, so they can get them hooked on it. Then they force them into a life of dependency, which includes making them sell their bodies in order to make them money and to support their habits."

"You're right, Alice!" Valerie agreed, with total disgust. "That is sick."

A set of headlights suddenly appeared, startling everyone.

Valerie knelt down beside Scott and gently lifted his head off of the cold concrete. As she squinted toward the bright lights, she breathed a sigh of relief, for she came to realize that the lights were coming from a police cruiser.

Scott and Valerie watched as a tall man emerged from the vehicle. He was carrying a club in one hand and a flashlight in the other.

"What's going on here, Rico?" The officer asked.

Rico shrugged his shoulders, and then, spat on the ground directly in front of the officer's feet.

The officer took his flashlight and surveyed the faces of everyone in the crowd. His light stopped when it reached Alice's face, which had turned a ghostly pale.

"Well, Alice!" The officer grinned, maliciously. "What's this? Are we about to deliver our little bundle of joy out here in the streets, among these low-life scum buckets?"

Alice glanced nervously, toward Valerie, who watched the proceedings, a bit confused.

"No, I'm not having our little bundle of joy out here in this filth. My friend over there is a nurse. She's going to help me, if it's any of your concern, Officer Dell."

"Officer Dell?" The man asked, as if he had just been wounded.

"Come on, now, Alice," Rico chimed in, bravely. "We all know that his name is Mortimer."

Suddenly, the entire gang began to howl in laughter, which infuriated the police officer to no end, as he began to approach them with his club waved high into the air, threateningly.

As the laughter subsided, Valerie stood up and walked over toward the officer and explained, calmly, "My friends, over there, need medical attention. Can you take us to a hospital?"

The man laughed, rudely, into Valerie's face, and replied, "I don't care about your friends, Missy! All I care about is that Alice, here, delivers this baby without any complications."

Valerie glanced over toward Alice and then down toward Shaun and Scott. When she returned her attention toward the policeman, she felt his hand wrap around her arm, roughly.

Valerie let out a slight cry of pain, as the man ordered her, "Go and get into the back seat of my cruiser. You too, Alice. We're going for a little ride."

Scott struggled to get to his feet, but he fell back down, helplessly.

Rico attempted to keep Alice from following the officer's orders, but he backed away, when the man flung his club over his head, as he warned, "I wouldn't try to be Rambo, if I were you, Rico."

Rico shot Officer Dell an incredibly angry glare, which only provoked the policeman into a fit of uncontrollable laughter.

"I have the power around here, Rico!" Officer Dell roared. "I would suggest that you and your little friends had better start to realize that and stop trying to resist me."

Rico and the other gang members decided to disperse and go home, while Alice reluctantly followed Valerie into the back seat of the police cruiser.

Rico turned his attention back toward Alice. He saw her helpless expression through the window, which caused him to feel a deep pain in his heart.

After walking away a safe distance, Rico shouted, "You'd better watch your back, Mortimer. Accidents happen to your kind in our 'hood'."

Scott watched, helplessly, as the police cruiser drove off into the night, leaving him and Shaun lying on the cold concrete, both writhing in pain.

Lincoln suddenly awoke in the middle of the night. Some unseen force caused him to sit upright in bed. His palms were sweaty, and he noticed perspiration forming around his forehead. He quickly got of bed. He knelt down and folded his hands. He began to pray, fervently, "Precious Lord Jesus, Glory be your name! I feel incredibly compelled to pray to you, Dear Lord. I am not aware of what is happening. All I know is that I need to come to you, Lord. I ask that you please guide my friends this night. Help them, Lord, as they attempt to reach out to others. You taught your disciples to go out and spread the gospel to those who are in need, Lord. This is truly a troublesome world we live in today, Lord. It is full of unbelievers, who live out dangerous lives, completely without the knowledge of your saving grace. They are walking in darkness, and their futures, without you, are so bleak. Their dismal lives only lead to destruction. Either their own or to the destruction of others. I come to you, tonight, Oh Lord, to ask you to watch and protect my friends as they go about your work. Please, Oh Lord, strengthen them and encourage them to go on. In these troubling times, we need your encouragement so badly. The enemy is strong and vindictive, but through the blessings of the Holy Spirit, we, as children of our Almighty God, can overcome anything Satan has to dish out against us. We love you, Oh Lord, with our hearts and with our very souls. We believe the truth as it was stated in your word. We believe that you were sent down from Heaven to save us from our sins. We truly believe that you died and that you were buried. We believe that you were raised from death on the third day, and that you now reign in Almighty Heaven beside God our Father. We also believe that someday you will return to judge the quick and the dead. We pray, Oh Lord, that you will find us worthy, as we glorify your name on high. In the precious name of Jesus Christ, we pray. Amen."

Scott, suddenly, began to attempt to rise to his feet. After stumbling a couple of times, he managed, somehow, to make it over to a nearby telephone booth.

Glancing back towards Shaun, Scott noticed that the boy was also attempting to get to his feet.

Fumbling in his pockets, Scott brought out a couple of dimes and nickels. After depositing some of the coins into the slot, he began to dial a number, praying that he was dialing it correctly, despite the throbbing pain in his head which was clouding his thoughts.

Scott thanked God, when a familiar, but slightly groggy voice, answered his call.

"Lincoln? This is Scott. I need your help, Buddy!" He cried.

Lincoln asked, "Where are you, Scotty?"

"I'm in an alley beside the Federal Building. Can you help me, Lincoln?"

Lincoln immediately replied, "I'm on my way, Buddy. Hang in there."

As Lincoln dressed, he shouted, "Thank you. Lord. Blessed be your name, Lord. Thank you, Jesus."

Scott hobbled back over to Shaun and told the boy, who was now sitting up, "Help is on the way, Shaun. I've called my good friend, Lincoln. He should be here in a few minutes."

Shaun began to rub his right arm while his face revealed the pain that he was experiencing.

"What exactly happened to you, this time, my little friend?" Scott asked.

Shaun began to explain, "I was minding my own business, leaning against this wall over here, when this limousine pulled up. It was huge......and.....clean. Well, this driver steps out. He's all decked out in this black and white tux. He had tails, a hat, and a cane....you know..... the whole nine yards. Well, I figured if the driver dressed like this, then his passenger must be loaded, so I accepted the driver's offer to get into the back of the limo. That.....was my first mistake. Once I got inside and the door was locked, one guy held me down while another one brought out this huge needle. They pushed up my sleeve and injected me with some junk. The next thing I know, someone else places this rag over my face. I remember smelling something like chloroform or something. The next thing I know, I'm losing all consciousness. Everything around me sort of begins to fade away into oblivion. I guess I passed out, because I don't remember them tossing me back out into the streets."

"When are you going to learn, Shaun, that these guys aren't just playing around? They really mean business!" Scott reasoned with the boy while trying to help him to his feet.

Shaun thought for a minute, and then he replied, "Not everyone out here is as crazy as those guys are."

"Yeah," Sam smiled, "but the crazies sure make up for it, though, Kid."

Shaun grinned, slightly, and then he began to look out in the direction that the police cruiser drove off into.

As if reading Shaun's mind, Scott shrugged and said, "I don't know what to make of that weird cop, either, Shaun. I only pray that Val and that pregnant girl will be all right."

Valerie glanced out of the rear window, as Officer Dell turned down a side street. She, then, glanced over at Alice and noticed that her face was turning a ghostly pale.

"Are you all right, Alice?" Valerie asked in a whisper.

Alice shook her head slowly, as she carefully watched the police officer.

"Well, ladies," Officer Dell announced, as he finally brought the cruiser to a halt, "home sweet home. Everyone out!"

Alice, reluctantly, obeyed the officer despite her great discomfort. Valerie, however, hesitated.

When Officer Dell emerged from the car, he stood by Valerie's window and bellowed, "That includes you, Nursie. Come on. Get out of the car. This will be your new home for awhile."

Valerie's head began to spin, as she struggled to understand just exactly what was unfolding before her. She finally snapped out of her confusion, when the police officer opened her door and reached in, grabbing her, roughly, by the arm.

Alice watched as the officer pulled Valerie from the cruiser, and she rushed over to her side. She screamed, "Mortie, don't treat her like that. She's a good person. She's my friend."

"Aw!" Officer Dell mocked. "She's your friend. How quaint! I really don't care, Alice. Now, the both of you had better get into that house, or I'll be forced to do something that I won't even regret."

A clap of thunder could be heard, a way off in the distance, as the two ladies entered the house. Alice flipped on a switch, which illuminated the living room. A long, leather couch sat along the opposite wall. An old coffee table stood in front of it. On top of the table stood a small statue.

Valerie noticed the stale smell of cigar smoke lingering in the air, as she walked around the room. The pale blue carpeting was wearing thin in spots. The wall, to the right, was splashed with some sort of liquid stain. Valerie assumed it to be from beer or something else.

"Why did you bring us here?" Valerie asked as she turned toward the officer, after he entered the house.

"Because, my dear," the officer explained, "you are going to deliver my baby."

Valerie quickly shot Alice a concerned glance, which confirmed the man's statement, as Alice turned her head away in shame.

Lincoln finally arrived on the scene, as Scott and Shaun stood waiting by the telephone booth.

They watched as Lincoln emerged from his small compact car. As Lincoln approached the two of them, Shaun, suddenly, began to freak out. He fell to the ground and began to convulse, uncontrollably.

Lincoln rushed to the boy's side, and attempted to calm him down.

Scott knelt down beside the boy, and explained to Lincoln, "He's been injected with something, possibly heroin."

"Good Lord!" Lincoln muttered under his breath.

After several minutes passed by, Shaun's tremors began to subside a little.

Lincoln prayed silently, thanking the Lord for his tender mercy.

As Lincoln continued to pray, silently, Shaun began to look around the empty streets. His eyes were suddenly filled with imaginary sightings, as he struggled to free himself from Lincoln's protective grip.

Coming down the streets, Shaun imagined, was a band of unruly bikers. Their long, greasy hair was flying in the wind as they headed down the street toward him. They were all drinking, and laughing, as they drew nearer and nearer.

Shaun became completely unnerved. He broke free of Lincoln, who was temporarily distracted by a flash of lightning that appeared, unexpectedly, nearby.

Scott watched, helplessly, as Shaun ran off into the night. A single drop of rain fell onto Scott's cheek, and ran down his face, like a tear.

As Chris arrived in front of Julia's apartment building, that next morning, he noticed her standing outside, waiting for him. She was, as Chris noticed, quickly putting out a cigarette in a nearby ash tray.

"This," Chris smiled, "ought to be interesting, Lord."

As Julia started to walk towards Chris' car, another car pulled up beside his. The driver happened to be Lucas.

"Hey, Chris," Lucas grinned, "what's going on here? Are you trying to steal my girl?"

Chris got out of his car, and walked over to Lucas' car, and replied with a smile, "Julia and I are going to church. Would you care to join us?"

Lucas scoffed, as he surveyed Julia's foiled attempt at trying to dress appropriately for church. Lucas laughed, "I wouldn't want to spoil the atmosphere, Chris."

Julia stepped closer to Lucas' window, and said, "I won't go if you don't want me to, Lucas."

Lucas laughed, once again, as he explained, "I've got no gripes about you going to church, Doll Face. It's just that you look pretty ridiculous in that tight little dress, and those shabby white shoes."

Julia hung her head in shame, as she began to experience the same sense of low self esteem that she had felt her entire life.

Witnessing her growing lack of self-confidence, Chris offered up some words of encouragement, as he said, "It doesn't matter what you wear to church, Julia. All that they ask for, is that you come to church with an open mind, and an eager heart to listen to God's word. You'll even see some people wearing blue jeans and short sleeve shirts."

Lucas commented, "Wow! Times, they are a changing."

"Are you coming, Lucas?" Julia asked.

Lucas suddenly became serious, as he replied, "No! I can't! I've got somewhere else to go."

Chris shrugged his shoulders and informed Julia, "We'd better get going if we're going to make the nine o'clock service."

Lucas watched as Chris and Julia got into the car. As they were backing out of the parking lot, he yelled, "Say a prayer for me, you two."

Chris smiled, waved his hand, and then he and Julia disappeared down the street.

Lucas got out of his car, and walked up the sidewalk which led to the front door of the building. He sat down on the steps, and began to stare off into space.

As Samantha pulled up into the parking lot of the church, she noticed that there was a crowd of people standing around someone.

"What on earth is going on, Samantha?" Helen asked, as she and her daughter climbed out of the car.

After they drew closer toward the crowd, Samantha realized that they were gathered around a man that she had once been engaged to.

When the man took notice of Samantha and her mother, he gently broke through the crowd and quickly wrapped his arms around them both and cried, "It's been ages. You two, simply, look gorgeous!"

Samantha and her mother both blushed slightly, from embarrassment, for the crowd of people were now staring at them, with anxious smiles.

"Oh, Erik!" Helen laughed. "You're still quite the ladies man."

"May I escort you two lovely ladies inside?" He asked, as he extended both of his arms.

Accepting his exquisitely charming offer, Samantha and her mother walked arm in arm toward the church entrance, followed by the others.

Just as the threesome was about to enter the church, a voice from somewhere in the crowd called out, "Helen! May I see you for a minute?"

Helen turned around and came face to face with her husband, Derek. She suddenly began to feel that ever familiar fear, right in the back of her neck, as she instinctively began to rub it with her right hand.

Samantha noticed the all too familiar look of false repentance upon her stepfather's face, as he obviously showed up on the scene to try and win back the affections and trust of her mother.

"Mama!" Samantha warned softly, "Be careful!"

"I just want to talk to your mother, Samantha," Derek explained politely. "That's all!"

Helen turned toward Samantha and Erik, and said, "Please excuse me. I'll only be a minute. I must speak to my husband."

Erik rubbed Samantha's elbow, reassuringly, as he ushered her inside.

Helen retreated down the stairs alongside her husband, where they found themselves alone, she asked, "Did those men find you, Derek? I'm sorry that I told them where you work. But they were threatening to hurt Samantha."

Derek's voice took on an extremely sympathetic tone, as he reassured his wife, "No, Helen, they didn't find me. Thankfully, I had a little bit of a warning before they entered the bar. I got out the back way, and I gave Ernie my notice. I quit the bar."

"You quit the bar?"

Derek attempted to appease his wife as he said, "I've decided to try and clean up my act, Helen. I'm going to try and find me a respectable job. I'm going job hunting tomorrow".

"That's wonderful, Derek!" Helen exclaimed, as she hugged her husband.

Lincoln spent the remainder of the previous night, attempting to calm Scott down, after taking him home. He had become very distraught after Shaun took off running in an extremely agitated manner.

Scott had watched, helplessly, as Lincoln tried to catch up with the young boy, but it became very obvious that the boy did not want to cooperate with anyone at that time.

Lincoln left Scott's house at seven o'clock that morning in order to give himself enough time to get ready for the morning service. Scott had declined to attend church that morning because of the throbbing pain that his minor concussion was causing him.

When Lincoln arrived at church, that morning, he noticed Chris and a young woman standing in a corner, whispering. Chris, apparently, was pointing something out to her from his Bible. The young woman appeared to be very interested. Their conversation seemed to be so intense, that they didn't even notice Lincoln when he walked up to them.

"Chris," Lincoln called out to his friend with an outstretched hand. "How are you doing?"

Chris looked up from his Bible and then he noticed the service was about to start, as he quickly introduced Lincoln to Julia.

"Where are you two sitting, Chris?" Lincoln asked, as they joined the other worshipers.

Chris explained, "Samantha is reserving us some seats, Lincoln. Come and sit with us."

Lincoln smiled as he followed Julia and Chris to the front row, greeting several people as he went along.

Pastor Mark Jenner stood in front of the congregation, with Bible in hand. He smiled warmly, as he addressed the congregation, "First of all, let me say good morning to you all. I am Pastor Mark Jenner and this is the Church of Faith in Christ. I, especially, would like to welcome our first time visitors. I pray that you will be blessed this morning as we worship our precious savior, Jesus Christ. I have the misfortune to report some sad news concerning two of our members. I was about to join them in holy matrimony, in the very near future. It seems their car struck a tree, two days ago. They both perished in the accident, which, by the way, is still under investigation. I wish to publicly bestow my sincerest sympathy to Sister Rosemary Harrison for the loss of her son, Adam, as well as to Sister Peggy Washington for the loss of her daughter, Denise. They will both be truly missed. While they walked down here on earth, they walked with God. Now, they are truly walking with God, for they both had confessed their sins and had accepted our Lord Jesus Christ as their Lord and personal savior. They also had participated in the holy baptism by water and they were also baptized by the Holy Spirit. We can rejoice that they are now in Heaven, where we shall see them again, someday."

Samantha glanced down toward Lincoln as he sat down and mouthed a question to him, silently, which was "Where are Scott and Valerie?"

Lincoln gave Samantha a look that told her he would explain everything to her, later.

The music director started to lead the band, that had assembled up front, before services began, in the first song, an old standard, which happened to be a favorite of Lincoln's.

Lincoln remembered how this song, which was entitled, "Victory in Jesus," had blessed him in the past. He also recalled the sweet days of his youth, when his grandmother used to sing this very song to him and his brothers.

Several members of the congregation sang along with the music, while others felt compelled to clap along with the rhythm. Others swayed to and fro, as the Holy Spirit began to descend upon the congregation.

Samantha turned towards her mother. She was seated next to Derek who had been persuaded to attend services seeing as he was already there. Samantha managed to give her stepfather a smile for she realized that as a Christian she should not fall into judgment of the man, and that no one is beyond saving, by the grace of God.

Erik glanced around the room and noticed that the Pastor's wife was standing at the entrance. She appeared to be nervous, as she attempted to sing along with the rest of the congregation. Erik gave her a smile, when she noticed him waving toward her. Maggie returned the greeting, and then she bolted out of the door, quietly. Valerie's hair was in slight disarray as she timed Alice's contractions which were erratically occurring throughout the night.

"You look like death warmed over, Nurse Valerie!" Alice said as she attempted a bit of humor in order to lighten the atmosphere.

"You don't look so hot yourself, Woman!" Valerie smiled, through the exhaustion.

"How much longer do you think it will be, Val?" Alice asked, as she winced at the pain.

Valerie replied, "Well, your last contraction occurred five minutes ago. If they continue to come more rapidly, I think we'll be ready to deliver before noon."

Officer Dell entered the bedroom, where Alice lay, followed by a small man with gray hair, and wire rimmed glasses.

"Hello, Alice," the elderly man greeted the young mother to be.

"Oh, no, Mortie!" Alice screamed. "Get that quack away from me. He isn't going to touch me or my baby."

Officer Dell was beginning to lose his patience when he replied, "All right! He'll just stand by in case there are any complications."

Valerie turned toward the elderly doctor and smiled, nervously, "I'm a nurse, Doctor, but I've never delivered a baby before."

The old man grinned, "There's nothing to it, Dearie."

Alice let out a scream, as another contraction began. This one seemed to be much stronger.

"How far apart are these contractions, now, Nurse?" The doctor asked.

Valerie glanced at her watch and answered, "Just over five minutes apart, Doctor."

"It won't be long now, Alice!" The doctor grinned.

Officer Dell decided to wait in the other room but before he left, he asked the old man, "Doc'! Would you like something to drink?"

The old man began to lick his dry lips as he answered, "Yes, Mort. Have you got any Irish whiskey?"

Officer Dell laughed, "Does an elephant have big feet?"

Pastor Mark began to read from the Bible, as the congregation listened intently, "Please turn to Hebrews Chapter 12 verses 5 through 9. I am reading from the New King James Version. It says, "And you have forgotten the exhortation which speaks to you as to sons "My son, do not despise the chastening of the Lord, Nor be discouraged when you are rebuked by Him; For whom the Lord loves He chastens. And scourges every son whom He receives. If you endure chastening, God deals with you as with sons; for what son is there whom a father does not chasten? But if you are without chastening, of which all have become partakers, then you are illegitimate and not sons. Furthermore, we have had human fathers who corrected us, and we paid them respect. Shall we not much more readily be in subjection to the Father of spirits and live?"

Pastor Mark noticed his wife reenter the church and watched her as she resumed her stance beside one of the ushers. He noticed that her arms were crossed in her characteristic manner. He shrugged off her strange behavior and then proceeded with his sermon.

"The word exhort means to urge by strong, often stirring argument, advice, or appeal. Therefore we are not to forget the times when we are corrected, as when a father urges his child against doing things which may harm him either physically, spiritually, or emotionally. We are chastised by our parents, as mere children, for our own welfare. So, when our Lord Jesus Christ chastises us from time to time, we should not rebel out of a sense of frustration or deep disappointment. Instead, we should rejoice in the fact that He loves us so dearly, that when we stray away from the paths of righteousness, He chooses to chasten us or purify us, if you will. If, we, as parents, fail to chastise our children from time to time, then we are being detrimental to our children. When a parent finds it necessary to punish their child, they are doing it for their own good. If a child goes on being unpunished, then they don't learn that what they have done can harm them. They feel free to continue down the path of destruction. We, even as adults, need the chastising from our Father in Heaven, when we begin to stray from the fold. And we are not to become proud or indignant, when the Lord corrects us. We should be in constant prayer. We should keep an open line of communication with our Heavenly Father, especially during those times when we feel we have strayed and when we feel the almighty sense of reprimanding by our Father. We as children of our earthly fathers have shown them the proper respect when we were corrected by them, so should it be the same, when our Lord expresses his love for us through his chastening."

The congregation began to stir, as Pastor Mark, said, "Let us pray. Dear precious Lord Jesus. Please continue to chastise us when we go astray. Sometimes, we get so caught up in this world of outright, blatant sin and moral corruption, that we sometimes, fail to realize nor fully appreciate your great gift of chastisement. You show us your everlasting love, through chastening. For if a father does not care when his child is doing something wrong, then he just turns his head and looks the other way, Lord. We thank you, Jesus, for never turning your eyes away from us, no matter how sinful we become. We thank you, Oh Lord, that you would renew our minds and spirits, as we continue our path towards you, and everlasting life. We also pray that if there is anyone here today who is still seeking your grace and forgiveness, who, as yet has not surrendered all to you, Jesus, that you would open their hearts, today, as we invite them to come forward and accept you, Oh Lord, as their Lord and personal savior. Amen."

Pastor Mark looked around the congregation, with a huge smile upon his face, as he offered the invitation, "Please, sing along with the choir, as I extend this invitation. This is truly a very joyous time. I feel there is someone out there who has heard the message, this morning, and that they have been truly blessed. I sense that they are feeling the almighty power of the Holy Spirit as it descends upon them like a huge warm blanket. Please, I pray, that you will respond to the Lord's plea, as He so loves you. Please, don't put it off. Come up front here and meet your Lord and Savior, Jesus Christ. Please, like the song says, Just as I am."

The choir reassembled in front and everyone began to sing, "Just as I am."

Pastor Mark looked around the room, and said, "If anyone here is still seeking forgiveness for their sins, please come forward and we will pray with you. If you have not accepted our Lord Jesus as your Lord and personal Savior, please let go of your pride or whatever else is holding you back. Our Lord is waiting to take you in his loving arms. He is ready to forgive you of your sins. He truly loves you. His love is totally unconditional. There are no strings attached to his love for you. All that he asks is that you hear him knocking at the door of your heart. He wants you to open your heart and allow him to enter in. He truly is an awesome God."

Suddenly, Julia's hands began to shake uncontrollably. Her eyes began to water. She reached out to Chris, and whispered, hoarsely, "Please help me. I need to go forward."

Chris' own eyes began to tear up, so badly, that he had to wipe away at them, for he knew what was taking place, in Julia's heart.

Samantha helped Chris as he lead a shaking Julia forward to the altar railing, where she knelt down in humble submission. Julia prayed aloud, as the choir began to sing much softer.

Julia's voice began to tremble and crack, as she cried, "Dear Lord, I am ready. I am ready to give it all over to you, Lord. I have sinned......badly. I am truly sorry, Lord. I didn't know...I just didn't realize......I love you Lord with all of my heart.......I love you with every fiber of my being...Please forgive me, Lord.......Please give me a brand new start. I can't go on living like I have. I need you to be my master, my savior. My life is no longer my own, Dear Jesus. I surrender all to you, Lord. Please help me, Jesus!"

Julia suddenly fell to the floor, as the Holy Spirit totally overcame her.

Several people from the congregation began to shout praises to the Lord, as Chris and Samantha watched Julia bask in the joy of the Lord.

Valerie's eyes suddenly began to tear up, as she looked heavenward. Whispering, she offered up praise, "Lord Jesus. You are truly merciful. Thank you, Lord. Thank you, Jesus."

Rosemary Harrison began to lean upon her friend Peggy's shoulder, while tears flowed down her face, rapidly. Peggy placed her arm around Rosemary's shoulders and just poured out her love and compassion for the grief stricken woman, bravely trying to control her own overwhelming emotions, as they watched Julia accept Christ.

Scott was, meanwhile, at home nursing his headache, when he suddenly fell to his knees at the foot of his bed, and began to pray fervently, for the safe return of Shaun. Tears began to flow down his cheeks as he felt the very presence of Jesus in the room.

Helen turned toward her husband. She felt his grip upon her hand growing tighter and tighter as if he were fighting some urge to do something. She noticed a strange look in his eyes that she had never seen before. As she attempted to rise from her seat to go forward to the altar railing, she felt Derek's grip get even tighter.

Shaun lay flat on his back in an alley behind an old abandoned warehouse. He was looking straight up towards the darkening skies. His blue eyes had turned extremely bloodshot as he stared upwards. Tears began to flow uncontrollably, as he realized that he was unable to get up off of the ground, for just moments earlier, both of his legs had been violently struck by a baseball bat that had been wielded by some unexpected assailant, who had attempted to rob him of money which he hadn't even been carrying.

Maggie stepped outside because she found herself beginning to hyperventilate for no apparent reason. As she stepped outside, the rain began to fall gently all around her. Erik joined her seconds later. They stood several inches away from each other, staring at one another, as their clothes, slowly, began to become dampened.

Lucas stood high upon a bridge railing. He looked down below at the water as it began to ripple, from the gently falling rain. He followed the river's current until he could see no further. Off to the right shore, Lucas noticed a couple of ducks swimming joyfully out towards the middle of the river. As he looked up into the darkening skies, he watched two gulls as they began to ascend toward the sky, together.

Julia finished her appeal and then with a tear stained face, she turned toward Chris and said, "Thank you, Chris."

Chris gave Julia a warm hug, as Samantha looked on, approvingly.

Suddenly, as a loud crack of thunder filled the air, Julia shouted, "We've got to find Lucas, Chris."

As Chris and Julia raced out of the church, Samantha began to look around for Erik. Helen approached Samantha with Derek holding onto her arm as if he were afraid to let go of it, and asked her, "Can you pick me up tonight, Dear? I'd like to attend evening services, too."

Samantha decided to stop looking for her former fiancee', as she replied to her mother, "Sure, Mama. But this doesn't mean you're returning home to him, are you?"

Derek tightened his grip upon Helen's arm as she reluctantly nodded in affirmation.

Pastor Mark approached Rosemary and Peggy, and placed a warm hand in each of theirs.

Rosemary was still crying, "Why? Why, Pastor Mark? Why did they have to die?"

Mark noticed his wife as she and Erik reentered the church. Out of the corner of his left eye, he watched them as they headed down the corridor which led to classrooms and offices.

"Our Lord has a plan for us all, Rosemary. It is not for us to question him, my dear. Think of it as a sort of blessing. After all, they didn't suffer, and they are now up in Heaven with our Father, giving praise to him in all of his splendid glory. Believe me, Rosemary, I know how much you are grieving, but Adam and Denise are very, very happy."

Rosemary turned toward Peggy, who finally allowed her own emotions to take their natural course, as she began to cry, uncontrollably.

Rosemary, suddenly, became the strong one, as she began to comfort her friend.

Lincoln approached Pastor Mark and asked him, "Did you get a chance to speak to Erik Masterson, Mark?"

"No!" Pastor Mark replied, rather bluntly.

Samantha walked up beside Lincoln and asked, "Where are Scott and Valerie?"

Lincoln explained, "I think our resident nurse is about to deliver a new born baby into this cold cruel world, and as for Scott, I think he is probably at home moaning and groaning."

Alice's forehead was beginning to perspire, heavily, as she began to push her baby through the birth canal. Valerie smiled, proudly, at the progress which her patient was making.

Officer Dell looked on from behind Valerie's left shoulder. He appeared to be very nervous at what was unfolding before him.

The old doctor sat in a nearby easy char, passed out from the whiskey that was supplied to him.

Valerie shouted, "Here it comes, now, Alice. I can see it's head and shoulders."

Alice puffed rhythmically, as she greatly anticipated this moment.

Officer Dell wiped the sweat from his brows as he cried out, "Well, I'll be!"

As she gently removed the child from Alice's womb, Valerie asked the policeman, "Well, you'll be what, Officer Dell?"

The officer watched as Valerie skillfully cut the umbilical cord.

Alice looked on and cried out, "Is it a boy or a girl, Nurse Valerie?"

Valerie said, "See for yourself, Alice," as she held the baby in the air.

Alice began to laugh hysterically, "A boy. It's a boy."

Officer Dell watched as Valerie cleaned the baby up, and then he commented, "Look, Alice, he's got your eyes."

Alice grinned, "You're right, Mort. And he's got your temperament. Listen to that scream. He's got a great set of lungs."

Officer Dell laughed, asking, "Are you implying that I have a big mouth?"

Alice giggled, "If the muzzle fits, Mortie, wear it in good health."

CHAPTER THREE

A SACRIFICE

Maggie and Erik entered the nursery, where a teenager was playing on the floor with a four year old boy, who was the last remaining child in the nursery. Maggie smiled down at the teenager and informed her, "Katie, services are over. Could you please take Johnny to his mother. She's gathering a few things from Pastor Mark's office."

"Sure, Mrs. Jenner!" Katie responded.

As Katie led Johnny out of the nursery, Maggie closed the door almost completely, as she whispered, "What are you doing back here, Erik? I thought you were going to stay in San Francisco."

Erik gave Maggie a warm hug, and laughed, "That's sure a fine welcome back to the man you almost married."

"I'm not the only sweet young thing you almost married, Erik Masterson."

Erik grinned proudly, "Oh, you must be referring to Samantha Taylor."

"I see you wasted no time in hooking up with her again, Erik," Maggie mumbled softly.

Outside of the nursery door, a figure lurked, quietly, in the corridor, listening to the conversation within.

"I see you managed to dig your finely manicured nails right into the heart of our young charismatic preacher, "Erik teased. "Tell me how you pulled that one off, Maggie."

Maggie boasted, "Mark fell head over heels in love me. I swear it was love at first sight for him."

"But what about you, Maggie?" Erik demanded, quite seriously. "I haven't heard any declarations of love on your part for the most esteemed clergyman."

A noise from out in the corridor brought the conversation in the nursery to an abrupt halt.

Lincoln and Samantha arrived at Scott's apartment directly following church to offer their pain stricken friend, some help.

As Scott opened the door, he groaned, "How was church, today?"

Samantha entered the apartment and replied, "A friend of Chris accepted Christ today."

Scott closed the door after Lincoln walked in behind Samantha.

"Boy, that bump on your head surely must be killing you, Scott." Lincoln empathized.

"Man!" Scott's voice trembled, "You're not kidding, Linc."

Samantha placed her purse down on a nearby table and said, "Come over here, Scott. Let me take a look at your head."

Scott attempted to laugh, but it only caused him more discomfort, as he asked, "What did you do over the weekend, Samantha? Did you take a crash course in home remedies?"

Samantha examined Scott's head, and concluded, "Well, whoever bashed you over the head sure didn't manage to knock out any of your precious sarcasm."

Lincoln laughed, "Scott just wouldn't be Scott without any of his trademark sarcasm."

Scott attempted a weak smile, as he asked his friends, "Just why did you two decide to come over here in the first place? I hope it wasn't to harass me, because I am really not up to it."

Samantha's voice took on a more serious tone as she explained, "We're worried about Valerie."

Scott sat down, slowly, upon his recliner, as he admitted, "I'm worried, too. I don't know anything about that police officer who abducted Valerie and that pregnant girl. My guess is that this guy probably wants Val to deliver that baby."

"But, why?" Lincoln asked. "Why won't he just let that girl have her baby in a hospital, like everyone else?""

"I don't know," Scott replied. "But, you two should have seen this guy. He didn't act like a cop. I think there's something fishy about him. He probably wants to do something unethical with that baby. Who knows? The guy might be married or something. He might even want to do some harm to the child."

Samantha took in a deep breath, let it out, slowly, and then she said, "We've got to find Valerie. This police officer sounds a little psychotic."

As thunder roared in the distance and raindrops fell meagerly, Chris and Julia walked up to Lucas' front door.

Chris watched as Julia began to turn her key in the door. Upon seeing the blank expression on Chris' face, Julia explained, "I used to feed his parakeets, while he went on his week long drinking binges."

Chris nodded and then he followed Julia into the apartment, which, upon entering, reeked with the smell of stale cigarettes and liquor.

"How can he live like this, Julia?" Chris asked, as he kicked a few beer cans out of his way.

"Believe me, Chris," Julia answered. "I haven't a clue."

Chris noticed a piece of paper hanging on the refrigerator door. It was pinned by a magnet in the shape of a rooster.

"Look at this Julia!" Chris called out as he waded through the several bags of garbage.

"A note?" Julia asked, slightly relieved.

"Yeah, I think so!"

"What's it say?" Julia asked, as she glanced over Chris' shoulder.

"It's my little buddy's scribbling all right. I'd recognize this scratching anywhere."

Julia repeated, "What does it say? Where is he?"

Chris read aloud, "Julia, my pet! I hope you had fun with my old drinking buddy turned preacher man. I think you would probably be much better off with a guy like him instead of me. You see, I'm no good. My daddy was right all along. He always told me that I would never amount to anything in this old world. I'm nearly thirty years old and I'm still acting like I did when I was a teenager. I haven't accomplished a blessed thing. Heck, my liver's probably shot by now. I don't know what to do anymore. I don't know where to turn. I'm hopelessly pathetic.

Daddy sure called it. I'm just glad that he isn't here to rub it in my face. Take care of yourself, Doll Face! Put in a good word for me with the big cheese up in the sky. That is, if you can think of any."

Julia's complexion suddenly turned a ghostly pale, as she whispered, hoarsely, "Chris! You.....you don't think that's what it sounds like.....do you?"

Chris shook his head confidently, as he replied, "No, Julia, he hasn't got the guts to do something like that. I've known Lucas for a long time, now. He's had a lot of bad breaks in his life. It's left him incredibly self pitying. He might be reaching out to us for attention or something. We can still go and try to find him, but I really don't think we need to push the panic button just yet."

Alice awoke from a short nap, and spotted Valerie curled up on a love seat, with her eyes closed. Glancing around the room, Alice suddenly got the tremendous urge to hold her new born son.

First, she noticed that the house was unusually quiet, and then Alice realized that she was too weak to climb out of bed, to go and look for her baby.

"Valerie!" Alice cried out.

Valerie sat straight up and screamed, "What is it, Alice? Is something wrong with the baby?"

Alice cried, "I don't know where he is. Where's Mort? Where's that crazy old doctor?"

Valerie recalled the nightmare that Alice's scream had interrupted.

In Valerie's dream, she was holding a newborn baby girl. Valerie was rubbing the baby's tender cheeks, when all of a sudden a masked surgeon started coming toward her with a blunt instrument. The doctor had the most evil look in his eyes, as he drew closer, and closer. Valerie attempted to climb out of bed, but she soon discovered that she was strapped in against her will.

The baby began to cry softly, as the surgeon drew within mere inches. Valerie stared in horror and disbelief as the surgeon prepared to drive, what now appeared to be a scalpel, into the precious child's tiny skull.

Valerie jumped up, a little wobbly in the legs, and called out, "Officer Dell! Dr. Adams!"

Alice continued to cry, "Maybe something happened to my baby while I was asleep."

Valerie reasoned, "I don't think Officer Dell wanted any records of that baby's existence."

Alice asked, "What are you saying, Nurse Valerie? Are you implying that he stole my baby for some reason?"

"I don't know for certain, but it seems logical to me, that he had me deliver your baby, in order to keep you out of a hospital where they would naturally record his birth."

"So, what exactly, are you suggesting, Valerie?"

Valerie heart ached, as she replied, solemnly, "I think he's probably selling it on the black market."

"No!" Alice screamed painfully.

Suddenly, the front door opened, and Officer Dell entered, smiling broadly. He said, "Look who woke up, Junior. Your lazy mother."

Alice's heart leaped for joy, as the officer entered the room and placed her baby into her outstretched arms.

Valerie eyed the policeman very suspiciously.

Maggie Jenner stepped into the pastor's office. She greeted him with a grin, as she said, "Hello, husband!"

Mark glanced up from the Bible and glared at his wife, and boldly defied her, as he said, "Katie Ross informed me that you kicked her out of the nursery, early, so that you could have some sort of private discussion with a certain man who goes by the name of Erik Masterson."

Maggie's grin quickly evaporated for she didn't like the tone of voice that her husband was using. It was a tone that he very seldom ever used, for he was, under normal circumstances, usually, a very calm and serene man.

"It wasn't all that early, Mark. Besides, the child's mother was just about to come for him, anyway."

"What did you and Mr. Masterson discuss, Maggie? Surely, it couldn't have been the ladies auxiliary meeting, now could it?"

Maggie replied, "No, Mark! We didn't discuss the ladies auxiliary meeting."

"Well, then, Maggie, my dear sweet wife," Mark continued, "were you and Mr. Masterson then discussing the upcoming woman's social, by any chance?"

Maggie sat down on a small wooden chair, and she began to rub her sweaty palms together, nervously, as she replied, "Mark! I have no idea where you are going with this insanely constructed interrogation, but I'd like to tell you here and now, I really don't appreciate it."

Mark laughed, strangely as he explained, "Don't you think that just because I am a man of God, that it doesn't automatically shield me from hearing idle gossip. Hasn't it ever occurred to you, Maggie, that certain members of our congregation take it upon themselves to look out for me, where you are concerned? They take it upon themselves to report to me when you are doing something that could be detrimental to my marriage."

"Your marriage?" Maggie's eyes grew wide in amazement. "Since when did our marriage become your marriage, Pastor Mark?"

"You're changing the subject, Maggie," Mark said angrily, "and you never answered my question about what you and Erik Masterson were discussing so secretly, in the nursery."

Maggie stood up, glared at her husband for a few seconds, and then stormed out, as she said, "You don't even deserve an explanation, Mark."

Samantha was talking on Scott's cordless telephone, while Lincoln stood at the stove stirring a small pan of soup, that he was preparing for Scott. Meanwhile, Scott was drawing a map of the areas where he believed that Shaun could possibly be located.

"Lincoln," Scott began thoughtfully, "do you remember seeing a small brick building on your way down Lakeside?"

"Sure!" Lincoln replied. "It was on the right hand side, next to some bakery."

"Exactly!" Scott shouted excitedly. "Some street kids use it to take shelter, sometimes. A nice old man lives there. He's sort of an eccentric, but he's got a heart of gold. He used to watch out for the street kids, you know, trying to keep them out of trouble. You might find Shaun there."

Samantha hung up the phone and turned to Scott with a smile, as she informed him, "Help is on his way!"

"Who is on his way?" Scott asked.

"I just called Erik Masterson," Samantha explained. "He'll meet us down there, Linc."

Scott shrugged his shoulders, and said, "Well, I guess Masterson's better than nobody."

Samantha laughed, "Are you worried that Erik might get his new wing tipped shoes dirty, Scott?"

Scott laughed along, "I'm sorry, Samantha. Tell Erik that I really appreciate whatever help he can be."

As a soft beeping noise sounded, Lincoln told them, "That's my pager."

Scott and Samantha watched as Lincoln retrieved his pager from his pocket.

"It's my grandmother!" Lincoln announced. "I completely forgot that I was supposed to go over to her place today. We're having dinner together. She's cooking a roast."

Scott quickly reassured Lincoln that he was by no means under any obligations to miss out on having dinner with his grandmother.

Lincoln thanked Scott and also apologized, saying that he would call him later on to get caught up on the progress.

After Lincoln bounded out of the door, Samantha stood leaning against the stove.

She smiled, with her arms crossed in front of her, as she said, "Well, I guess it's a good thing Erik will be helping us, after all."

Scott shook his head and muttered, "Lord, help us!"

Rico walked along a tall building, whistling softly, as he, nonchalantly, surveyed several trash heaps. Randomly, he stuck a long stick into a bag, searching for nothing in particular.

Suddenly, he stopped digging, when he heard a moaning coming from behind a steel garbage can.

At first, as experience dictated, Rico's initial impulse was to get himself out of Dodge. He prided himself in bravery so he decided to investigate.

As he cautiously, peered around the can, Rico discovered a body lying, helplessly, on the ground.

"What's up with you little man?" Rico asked.

A few seconds later, Rico realized that he recognized the body to be that of the boy he saw the other day, when Alice and that other lady were abducted by that crooked policeman.

"Hey!" Rico shouted. "I know you! What happened to you this time, little man?"

Shaun managed a grin, as he said, "You sure couldn't care less the other day, Man!"

Rico explained, "I would have helped you, Man. But I've got a reputation to maintain. You know, all of my comrades were standing around."

Shaun laughed, slightly, "I guess I'll keep that in mind, Pedro. From now on, when I need you to be a good Samaritan, I'll try and make sure your buddies are busy doing something else."

Rico held out his hand, revealing a different ring on each finger.

Shaun explained, painfully, as Rico helped him to his feet, "I think my legs are either broken or maybe just badly bruised. I don't think I can walk, Pedro."

Rico laughed, as he placed Shaun's arm around his neck, for support, "Little man! Why do you insist upon calling me Pedro? I am Rico! Rico Sanchez!"

Shaun giggled nervously, "Sure! Whatever you say, Pedro!"

Pastor Mark sat in his office, studying the Bible, when a gentle knock was heard.

"Come in, please!" He called out, while folding his reading glasses.

Rosemary Harrison entered, and said, "I'm sorry, Pastor Mark, but I need to speak to you about Peggy Washington. I'm really worried about her. As you know, she had been keeping all of her emotions inside of her. That was, until this morning, following services."

Pastor Mark indicated a chair for Rosemary to sit down upon.

Mark said, "As you probably already know, Rosemary, everyone has their own ways of coping with grief. You were unable to contain your grief from the very start, but you were remarkable when the going got tough for Peggy, all of a sudden. I was very proud of you."

Rosemary took in a deep breath and then let it out slowly. Raising her hands up in the air, helplessly, she explained, "I don't know how to help her get through this, Pastor Mark. Ever since her breakdown this morning, I can't seem to get her to snap out of it. All that she does is stare into space. Her eyes are continually tearing up, and she won't eat. She won't respond to anything or anyone. She's sort of like a zombie or something. It just breaks my heart in two, seeing her like this."

"I know what you mean, Rosemary," Pastor Mark concurred. "Under normal circumstances, Peggy Washington is the most vibrantly, loving woman I ever met. This tragedy has just seemed to sort of totally destroy her."

"What can we do for her, Pastor Mark?"

Mark took Rosemary's hand into hand and said, after closing his eyes, "We can pray......Dear Lord, we come to you at this time for you said that whenever two or more gather in your name, then your presence would truly be felt. We pray to you for our friend Peggy Washington. She is suffering so much at the loss of her daughter Denise. Peggy needs your divine guidance to get her through this tragedy. We are calling upon you to show her some of your tender mercy. She loves you Lord, with all of her heart, but I fear her faith may be taking a brutal shaking up. Please, show her your love. Reveal to her that you have a plan for each and everyone of us. Help her to cope with her sudden and totally unexpected loss, as she must find a way to get on with her life. So many people have been blessed by Peggy's wonderfully good nature. She has always been there for others when they were going through rough times. I pray to you, Dear Lord, that you would send someone Peggy's way, who can have an equally positive effect upon her. She deserves to find happiness and peace of mind again. In Jesus' name we pray. Amen!"

Rosemary's eyes began to tear up, as she held onto Pastor Mark's hands, tightly.

Samantha climbed out of her car, looking around, nervously, for Erik. She glanced at her watch and realized that he wouldn't be there for another twenty minutes or so. As she walked along Lakeside Avenue, she felt the cool breeze that was coming off of the lake.

As she turned up her collar, she noticed a man in the distance. He was helping a young boy, who appeared to be injured.

"Excuse me!" Samantha called out.

The man stopped, looked around toward Samantha, and shouted, "Leave us alone, Lady! Everything is under control."

Samantha sprinted toward them, and as she neared them, she asked, "Have either of you seen a policeman around here?"

The man replied, "Hey, Lady, we try to avoid the cops, you know what I'm saying?"

Samantha looked at the boy and asked, "What's wrong with your little boyfriend?"

Rico gently placed Shaun down upon the concrete and glared at Samantha and asked, "What are you trying to say, Lady? You trying to say I'm a freak?"

Samantha explained, "No! I just said that in order to get your attention."

Rico grinned, "Very smart, Lady! And, now that you've got my attention, what do you want?"

Samantha explained, "I'm looking for a friend of mine. She's got auburn hair. She stands about five feet four. She's a nurse. I was told that she was forced into a car with a pregnant girl, so that she could deliver the baby. Do you two know anything about it?"

Rico shot Shaun a warning glance, as the boy attempted to speak up.

"You know something, don't you, Boy?" Samantha made a wild guess.

Watching Rico's eyes, Shaun shook his head, reluctantly.

Samantha glanced toward Rico and realized that he was calling the shots.

Taking another wild guess, Samantha asked Shaun, "Are you Shaun, by any chance?

Shaun nodded, quickly, before Rico could stop him.

"Oh, Little Man! You blew it, Man! We don't know who this lady is. She could be some kind of undercover policewoman."

Samantha laughed, as she said, "You are one paranoid dude!"

Rico suddenly felt he could trust Samantha, so he held out his hand, as he said, "My name is Rico Sanchez. If you're looking for that nurse and Alice, I'd like to help you. Alice is a friend of mine, and I don't trust Mort, one bit."

Samantha asked, "Who is Mort?"

"He's the slime ball who took your friend away in his police cruiser, against her will."

Samantha smiled, as she said, "Now, we're making some headway. Where does this crazy cop live?"

Rico shrugged. Shaun winced in pain. Samantha looked up toward heaven and rolled her eyes, helplessly.

While he was climbing into his car, Erik explained, "I've got to meet Samantha, downtown, Maggie. It's some sort of emergency, involving Valerie Rhodes."

Maggie pleaded, before Erik could close his car door, "Don't go to her, Erik. I need to talk to someone who understands. Mark doesn't understand me. You do. You're the only one who really knows me."

Erik attempted to close his door, but realized that it was impossible, because Maggie's left leg was blocking it, strategically.

"Maggie, I can talk to you, tonight, following church. I promise. We'll talk for as long as you need to."

Maggie threatened desperately, "I'll tell Samantha about Tyler, if you don't cooperate with me, Erik."

Erik frowned, looked at his watch and threw his hands up in the air, helplessly, as he said, "I give up, Maggie. You win! Even though it would surely cause a huge scandal in the church if you started telling people about Tyler. I don't think your marriage could withstand the pressure. And, frankly, my dear, I think that if our little secret came out, it would spell the end of your husband's career."

Maggie called Erik's bluff. She said defiantly, "As for my marriage, Erik, if it's any of your concern, it's been rocky from day one. Being married to the holier than thou Pastor Mark hasn't exactly been a Fourth of July picnic."

"Do you mean to tell me, that the holy man doesn't cause you to see fireworks?"

"Hardly!" Maggie frowned.

"Well, my dear," Erik said, "I really must get going."

Regretfully, Maggie allowed Erik to close his door, but she refused to step back. After Erik motioned with his hands for her to back away, she finally obliged. Maggie watched as Erik drove off down the street, until his car was completely out of sight.

Julia and Chris felt very uncomfortable as they entered Lucas' favorite drinking establishment, with the hopes that they would find him wallowing in a bottle of beer, in some remote, lonely corner of the room.

A man, who was obviously, already overserved, stopped Julia and slurred, "Where's your drunker half, Julia?"

"I don't know, Eddie! I'm looking for him. Got any ideas?"

Eddie's breath was causing Chris' stomach to churn, as he glanced around the room, surveying the surroundings with a renewed sense of pity for all of the lost souls sitting around drowning out their own individual sorrows.

"Forgive them, Lord," Chris thought silently, "they don't know what they're doing."

Eddie laughed loudly, "Oh, Doll Face, I've got plenty of ideas, but none of them are about Lucas. Do you know what I mean, Honey?"

Julia handled Eddie's rude advances with such skill, that it left Chris totally in awe of her. He began to realize what a remarkable young woman she really was. Julia gently pushed by Eddie and leaned against the bar, in order to get the attention of the bartender.

"Tony, has Lucas been in here today, yet?"

The bartender, a young man with prematurely gray hair growing around his temples, replied, "No, Julia, Lucas hasn't shown up here, yet. Should I tell him that you're looking for him, if he shows up, later?"

Julia nodded her head, and muttered to the bartender, "Would you? Thanks, Tony!"

Chris was beginning to grow very uncomfortable, for there was a time when he used to be a regular here, himself. Despite the renewing of his spirit, and the incredible turn his life had taken ever since he accepted Christ, two years ago, Chris still felt all of the old desires and memories of his drinking days, come flooding back to him in torrents.

Julia took one look at Chris, and she could sense his dilemma. She asked him, "Would you like to blow this lemonade stand, Chris?"

Chris nodded, at once, and he allowed Julia to lead him out of the door.

Once they were outside, Chris took in a deep breath of fresh air. He asked Julia, "How can they breathe in there? The smoke was so thick, I thought that I was going to pass out."

Julia laughed, "That's one habit that I won't be missing. With Jesus' help, I am going to attempt to kick my smoking habit once and for all."

Chris gave Julia an instinctive hug, as a show of support.

Julia, suddenly remembered something, as she gently broke away from Chris' embrace.

"What is it, Julia?" Chris asked.

Julia stared off down the street and said, "Lucas loves watching the ships out on the lake. Maybe he went to the lake to clear his mind."

"Well, we can take a look," Chris offered, as they headed for his car.

Valerie watched from a distance, as Alice fed her son. Smiling, proudly, Valerie said, "Motherhood must feel great, Alice."

Alice looked up from her baby and said, "Yes, it does, Valerie. You ought to give it a try, some time."

Valerie's smile immediately vanished as she slumped down in a chair.

"What's wrong, Val?" Alice asked.

Valerie explained slowly, "I hardly ever talk about this to anyone, because it still hurts too much."

Alice adjusted her baby a bit, and then she asked, "What's wrong?"

Valerie stared out of the big picture window, and watched as the rain gently struck the glass, and then she began to reveal a memory from her past.

"I was only fifteen years old, when I was attacked by a man. He had broken into our house, late one night. My parents were attending one of their many social functions that night. Well, I was just beginning to doze off, when all of a sudden I heard a noise in the living room. I grabbed my robe and before I had time to put it around my shoulders, I felt this man grab me by the hair with one hand and with the other, he covered my mouth. I tried to scream, but I wasn't able to. The man was much too strong. I couldn't fight him off."

Alice listened intently, as Valerie continued, "Well, I'll spare you the gory details of his attack, because it was very brutal and violent. He raped me, and I felt totally violated. He threw me down on my bed, and he warned me not to report it to the police because he said if I did, he would return and murder my parents."

Alice held her baby up against her right shoulder in order to burp him, as she felt her eyes begin to water.

Valerie continued, "For the longest time, I didn't tell anyone what had happened to me. It was too embarrassing and painful. I tried and tried to erase it all from my mind. There was a time when I even tried to convince myself that it never even happened. Well.....as time went on....certain changes began to take place inside of my body. A couple of months later, while I was sitting at home talking to my mother, I began to feel a little dizzy. She rushed me to the emergency room, because she said I looked like death warmed over. After a few tests were given to me at the hospital, it was discovered that I was eight weeks pregnant. My mother demanded to know who the father was. My own father went totally ballistic, at the thought of my having been with someone at my age."

"Did you have the baby?" Alice asked, as she laid her son beside her on the bed.

Valerie shook her head, slowly, while still watching the falling rain, outside.

"Did you have an abortion, then?"

Valerie turned toward Alice and her baby. After a moment, she replied, "I wanted to have the baby, even though I had been raped. I always loved babies. I was always baby sitting. I never baby sat for the money. I always watched other people's kids for them because I loved children. My father forced me to go through with the abortion. My mother wanted the decision to be my own. She said that she would support any decision that I made. But, my father had to have his way. He forced me to go through that awful procedure, where they stuck some long sharp instrument inside of me, as they sucked my baby's brains out of her skull."

"It was a girl?" Alice asked.

"Yes, it was a girl."

"How old would she have been, by now?"

Valerie stared at Alice and, without blinking, she replied, "She would have been around nine years old."

"I'm so sorry, Valerie," Alice cried, as she picked up her son and gave him a small squeeze.

Valerie continued, "The whole procedure was so cold and cruel. I was totally depressed for about the next four years after my father had given those butchers permission to murder my baby. My father and I never got along with each other after that. I began to hate him, with this relentless rage. My mother and he eventually got a divorce. My father left the state, married someone else, had another daughter by her, and I completely lost all contact with him, ever since. That is, until I started sending him birthday cards and Christmas cards. But, no matter what I did, he never reciprocated."

"It's almost like he wanted to just forget that you even existed," Alice suggested, politely.

"Exactly!"

Valerie turned back toward the window and watched a dog run through a puddle, as he hurried along the street.

Erik finally reached his destination, parking his expensive foreign car beside Samantha's domestic car. After climbing out of his car, Erik glanced around the deserted streets, but was unable to spot anyone.

As Erik was about to yell out Samantha's name, a voice from behind him, shouted, "Hey, you in those alligator shoes! Are you here to meet up with some chick named Samantha?"

Erik quickly reeled around and found a gang of young kids from the neighborhood. Instinctively, Erik stuck his key into his car door, and turned it to make sure that it was locked.

"Yes, I am! Have you seen her?" Erik asked suspiciously.

"Yeah, we can take you to see her, but I wouldn't leave your car parked there. You're liable to lose your fancy hubcaps."

Erik asked, "Can I pay one of you to stay here and watch it until I return with Samantha?"

The gang member with a patch over one eye laughed, as he said, 'I'll watch it for you, Lord Fauntleroy......but my services don't come cheaply. How much are those caps worth to you?"

Erik frowned, as he attempted to place a price on his hubcaps.

"How does thirty dollars grab you?"

The boy with the patch laughed once again, as he said, "Per hubcap!"

"That's highway robbery!" Erik cried out in total disbelief.

"Hey! I might have to risk my life in order to save your precious hubcaps from suddenly becoming public property."

The entire gang started howling with laughter, as Erik opened up his wallet to count out his cash.

Suddenly, a more familiar voice was heard, who asked him, "Erik, what are you doing?"

Erik turned around and came face to face with Samantha and two guys who he didn't recognize.

"What kept you, Skippy?" Samantha's younger companion asked.

"Skippy? " Erik asked.

Once again, the gang of juveniles roared with laughter.

Samantha attempted to disguise her own amusement by pretending she had a cough.

"Are you laughing at me, Samantha Taylor? Just who are your new found friends, anyway? Are they rejects from the Dead End Kids the next generation?"

Samantha suddenly realized that the gang was no longer finding Erik amusing, for silence had suddenly begun to prevail over the area.

"They're really good guys, Erik. That is, after you get to know them."

Erik scowled at the gang and they, in turn, sneered back at him.

Samantha turned toward Rico, who was still helping Shaun stand up.

"Rico, does anyone here know where this crooked cop lives?"

Erik put away his wallet and interrupted, as he exclaimed, "Crooked cop! You never told me anything about a crooked cop, Samantha."

Rico ignored Erik's outbursts as he asked his friends, "Do any of you know where Mortimer lives?"

Just as everyone was thinking about the question, a police cruiser drove by, at lightning speed.

Rico shouted, "There goes Mortimer, now."

Samantha shouted, excitedly, "Quick, Erik, get into your car and follow him......hurry up. He's stopped at that traffic light."

Erik, without thinking of the possible consequences, obeyed Samantha's command, by quickly unlocking his car doors, and climbing in behind the driver's seat.

Samantha helped Shaun into the back seat, while Rico pushed Erik over.

Rico shouted, "Samantha, I'll catch that dirty no good cop."

Erik cringed, while Rico made the tires squeal, as they sped off down the street.

Lincoln pulled up to his grandmother's old farmhouse, and sat behind the wheel to take in the peaceful surroundings.

"Lord, this is the life!" Lincoln grinned.

The front door to the farmhouse flew open, as an elderly woman with a cane stepped out onto the porch.

"Is that you, Lincoln, my boy?" The woman shouted. "My eyesight isn't what it used to be, you know."

Lincoln climbed out of his car, and called out, "It's me all right, Gram'."

"Come over here and give me some of that brown sugar, Boy," she laughed. "It's been far too long in between visits."

Lincoln bounded over toward the porch, sprinted up the steps, hugged his grandmother, and then planted a kiss upon her left cheek.

"How's that, Gram'?" Lincoln asked.

"It'll do, for starters," she giggled. "Now sit down here beside me on my swing and tell me what's been happening in your life, lately. Have you found some sweet young thing to share your life with, yet? You're not getting any younger, you know, Lincoln."

Lincoln helped his grandmother sit down on the swing, and then he joined her, taking her hand in his.

"No, Gram'!" Lincoln replied. "I'm still searching for her. She's out there somewhere. It's going to take a little more time and patience."

Lincoln's grandmother smiled, as she attempted to focus her weakening eyes upon her favorite grandson.

"Well," she smiled. "I'm running out of patience. I just want my boy to be happy. That's all."

Officer Dell entered his house unannounced and startled Alice and Valerie as they were attempting to change the baby's diaper.

"I was being followed, Ladies, but I think I lost them. My police training sure comes in handy from time to time."

Valerie turned around and came face to face with the officer and informed him, bravely, "Junior, here, needs to go to a hospital and get a professional checkup."

Alice pleaded, "Please, Mort. Have a heart. There might be something wrong with him, and we wouldn't even have a clue."

"There's not a thing wrong with Junior. He's as healthy as his old man."

"Oh, Mort. You're as stubborn as a mule!" Alice cried.

"Oh, so now you're into name calling, Alice. I think that this here nurse has been a bad influence on you. What has she been filling your head with?"

Alice held on to her baby, tightly, for Mort was watching him in a strange way, that frightened her to death.

Valerie attempted to reason with the officer, for her gut feelings were telling her that Alice's heart was about to be broken.

"Why won't you allow Junior to be examined by a real doctor?" Valerie asked.

"It's none of your business, Nursie," Mort replied.

Bravely, Valerie got into Mort's face, and said, "Hey, Buster! You made it my business, the minute you forced me into your cruiser."

"Well, we don't need you anymore. Besides, it probably was some of your friends who were trying to tail me, just awhile ago. They could spoil everything, if they discover where I live."

"Just what exactly is your master plan for Alice and little Junior, Mort?" Valerie demanded to know.

Alice warned, "Take it easy, Valerie."

Mort laughed, cruelly, as he said, "Listen to the little Mama, Lady. She knows about my temper, first hand. Go ahead! Ask her how she got that bruise on her left arm."

Valerie turned toward Alice, who attempted to hide the hideous spot on her arm.

Valerie shook her head in disgust, as she turned back toward the police officer, and asked him, "Just what exactly, is keeping me from reporting you to the authorities? They could take your badge for committing domestic abuse and for kidnapping."

Mort laughed, once again, as he pretended to be shaking in his boots, as he explained, "I have an impeccable record with the police department. In fact, I have several awards, and I only have two more years until retirement. It will have to come down to your word against mine. The media will crucify you, and make a hero out of me."

Valerie returned to the sofa, and continued to stare out of the window.

Rico laughed, as he sat outside of Mort's house. He explained to the others, "That sucker thought he lost us, but I only pretended to stop at that red light. He didn't notice it when I coasted through it. Man, he's not as bright as he thinks he is."

Samantha glanced up at the house where the police cruiser sat, and wondered if Valerie and Alice were inside or not.

Erik started to get out of the car, when Rico stopped him.

"Wait a minute, Urban Cowboy! This isn't Disneyland. Old Mortie's got a gun. He carries it wherever he goes, and he's not afraid to use it when he feels himself backed up against a wall."

Samantha whispered, "We've got to do something, Rico. We can't just wait here, doing nothing."

Julia searched the beach for any signs of Lucas, but her search proved to be unsuccessful. After she returned to Chris' car, she found him saying a silent prayer.

"Who are you praying for, Chris? Was it about Lucas?"

Chris nodded, "Yes, I prayed that Lucas would somehow find some sort of peace within himself."

"That's truly beautiful, Chris," Julia commented.

"Well," Chris asked, "where do we look next?"

Julia shrugged and said, "I don't know!"

Lincoln asked his grandmother, "Gram', how would you like to come to church with me, tonight? Do you remember Peggy Washington and Rosemary Harrison? Well, their children were killed last week in a car accident, just weeks before they were about to be married to one another. I thought that you might like to offer up your condolences to them."

A single tear of compassion developed in the elderly woman's right eye, as she felt the pain that those two women must be feeling. Dabbing at her eye, with a small handkerchief, the woman nodded that she would indeed like to be there tonight.

Lucas paid a man, wearing a gray trench coat, a wad of money, and in return, he was handed a small package. Lucas watched as the man disappeared around a corner, and then he turned around and headed off down the street in the opposite direction. As he came to an intersection, Lucas proceeded to walk across the street, completely oblivious to the oncoming traffic that was forced to veer around him in order to avoid running into him.

When he finally reached his apartment, Lucas sat down on the steps and began to carefully unwrap the package.

Chris suggested, "Let's try his apartment one more time, Julia. I have this feeling that he has gone back home, again."

Julia glanced at her watch and said, "It's almost time for church, Chris. Let's check on him after church."

"All right!" Chris agreed. "I hope some more miracles occur, tonight."

Maggie sipped at the contents of the bottle in her hand, as she sat in the smoky room. She glanced nervously, around the room, hoping that she would not be recognized. So far, she felt safe in this environment, for she was surrounded by complete strangers, who did not expect anything from her.

Rosemary led Peggy into the church, and they sat down beside one another, while a man placed offering envelopes on each of the chairs.

Rosemary watched her friend with immense compassion, for she was still looking completely expressionless, as if she had lost all of her senses. Tears began to flow down Rosemary's face as she attempted to get Peggy to speak.

Helen went to answer the door, while Derek went to the bathroom to shave. Just before she opened the door, Helen smiled, contentedly, at the thought of Derek's agreeing to take her to church tonight, if Samantha didn't arrive in time.

As she unlocked the door, it flew open, knocking her to the floor. Derek came running into the room, with razor in hand and shaving cream all over his face. His expression turned to sudden horror, as he came face to face with a gun toting hit-man.

Mort was becoming completely unnerved by Valerie's constant badgering, so he walked over toward Alice and watched her, as she held her baby.

Valerie's nerves were beginning to unravel, as her vibes of impending heartbreak began to get stronger and stronger.

Samantha was growing quite impatient, as she got out of the car, despite Rico's objections. Erik followed Samantha, as she slowly made her way up the sidewalk. Meanwhile, Shaun began feeling as if he was going to die if he didn't get a fix. Suddenly, his addiction overwhelmed any sort of physical pain he was feeling, as he started to crawl out of the back seat.

"Hey! Where are you going, Little Man? You still have a bum leg," Rico cried out, in vain.

Rico watched as Shaun limped down the street toward the direction from which they had just come.

Maggie sipped the last drop from her bottle and then she motioned for her server to get her another one. After she was, once again served, Maggie took a good long sip, ran her tongue along her lips, and then, she spotted a boy who was about four years old. He walked right up to Maggie, and asked her, "Have you seen my mother, Lady? I can't find my mother."

Maggie asked the boy, "Tyler? Are you my Tyler? Answer me boy! I think I'm your mother!"

Valerie confronted Mort, once again, "You've got to stop this right now, Mort, before it's too late. Junior may need medical attention. You don't want to endanger your son. Please let me take him and Alice to the hospital."

As he looked out the window Mort began to panic. Samantha and Erik were closing in on him. He shoved Valerie out of the way, as he shouted, "They won't take me alive. I'll go out shooting."

Alice cried out, "No, Mort!"

Valerie jumped onto Mort's back as he attempted to jerk Junior out of Alice's arms.

Lucas pulled out the contents of the small package and examined it, carefully. He, then sat down on the steps which led to his apartment building. Glancing around, making sure that the streets were deserted, so that he would not be interrupted, Lucas placed the loaded revolver in his mouth and pulled the trigger.

Julia and Chris entered the church and walked up to Rosemary and Peggy. Chris held Peggy's hand for a few minutes, winked, knowingly, toward Rosemary, and then he and Julia took their seats in the front row.

Alice cried out as Valerie fell to the floor, and again, when Mort kicked the nurse in the side with tremendous force.

"Give me that baby, Alice. He's mine, and he's going to earn me a great deal of money."

Alice cried, uncontrollably, as she was forced to relinquish her baby to the madman.

After he got the baby in his arms, Mort gave Valerie another swift kick.

As the doorbell sounded, Mort got completely unnerved. He began to pace the floor, trying to decide what to do.

Alice cried, "Mort, don't do this. Give my baby back to me. Please!"

Mort shouted, "Shut up, Alice! I can't think straight."

Samantha stood at the door, wondering what to do, when Erik came to her side. When there was no response to the doorbell, Samantha asked Erik, "Have you ever kicked a door in, before?"

Erik scoffed at the idea, looked down at his expensive shoes, cringed, and then he said, "What the heck? They're only shoes."

Samantha stood back, as Erik gave the door one mighty blow, causing it to open far enough for Samantha to enter.

Maggie swallowed hard, as she finished another bottle. The boy still sat across from Maggie as she continued to talk to him.

"Tyler, you really have turned into a handsome young man. Are those people you live with taking good care of you?"

The boy nodded, as he asked her, "Why did you give me up?"

Maggie's eyes began to water, as she struggled for an answer.

The boy repeated his question, "Why did you give me up, Mommy? Didn't you love me? Why don't you love me, Mommy? Was I a bad baby?"

Maggie began to sob, as she watched the boy's expression turn to immense sorrow.

Maggie cried, "You were a good, good baby, Tyler. I had to give you up. Your father wouldn't marry me."

The boy began to cry, softly, "So......you could have still kept me for yourself."

Maggie watched as the boy slowly faded away into the smoky air before her.

"Tyler!" She cried out, miserably. "Come back to me. I love you, Tyler."

The server returned to Maggie's table and asked her, "What's wrong, Ma'am?"

"That little boy! Where did that little boy go to?" Maggie asked, while wiping away the tears from her eyes.

The server's face contorted into a look of utter confusion at Maggie's question as he replied, "No one under twenty one is allowed in this establishment, Ma'am. Ernie, at the door sees to it that no one sneaks in here who doesn't belong. I guarantee you, Ma'am, no little boy has ever set foot in here."

Suddenly, without warning, a memory which Maggie had managed somehow to suppress, came flooding back to her with full force.

She remembered driving along a street, just after dark. She had been driving a short distance, when she felt herself nodding off at the wheel. She had discovered, to her horror, that she was on the wrong side of the street, when she spotted an oncoming car. She had panicked at the last minute. She had been temporarily blinded by the oncoming headlights, that she couldn't decide whether or not to get back onto the right side of the road. Making a last minute decision, she remembered veering over to her own side of the street. She recalled the screeching tires and the sound of the oncoming car, as it struck a nearby tree. She had climbed out of her car to investigate the accident.

"Oh my God!" Maggie gasped. "I killed Adam and Denise!"

Shaun stumbled along the street, painfully. He was becoming very tired, as he ventured onward. But his intense desire to have his addiction satisfied drove him on.

After he stumbled along for about five minutes, he came to rest upon a set of steps, which were only dimly illuminated. As he sat down upon the steps to rest, his arm came down upon someone's leg, which startled him to no end.

Jumping up, Shaun cried out, "Are you drunk or something, Man? What's wrong with you?"

As Shaun looked closer, he discovered that he was speaking to a lifeless body, who's head had been blown off by a revolver. Shaun struggled against vomiting, as he fell back down the steps in a heap, crying like a little child.

Mort hid behind the door that Erik had managed to loosen from it's hinges on his first try. After Erik and Samantha entered the house, Mort proceeded to run outside, toward his police cruiser, in which he had placed a small carrier.

Valerie screamed to Erik, "He's taken Alice's baby. Go after him."

Erik turned around, and boldly headed out the door, to find the police officer peeling out of the driveway, clutching the baby in his arms.

Erik watched as Rico took off after the policeman in hot pursuit.

Erik returned to the house, and announced, "My car is being driven by a young hood. As we speak, he is chasing that crooked cop, at break neck speed. Valerie, can you say a prayer for my car's safe return?"

"Oh, Erik!" Samantha cried.

Maggie stumbled up the steps of the church and deliberately avoided contact with several parishioners, as they attempted to greet her. Pushing past them, Maggie made her way to her husband's office, where he sat praying, as was his custom, directly prior to services. Without knocking, Maggie made her way into his office, crying, uncontrollably. Mark rose from his kneeling position, and rushed to his wife's side.

"What's wrong, Maggie? Are you ill?" He asked.

Maggie struggled to keep from slurring her speech, and for the first time during her marriage to the pastor, she didn't try to disguise her breath which reeked with the smell of alcohol. Maggie's expertly applied makeup was now running down her cheeks as she continued to cry.

Mark repeated his question, "What's wrong, Maggie?"

Maggie cried, "Don't you get it, Mark? Can't you smell my breath? Are you so inattentive to my needs that when I go on a drinking binge, that you don't even notice my breath?"

Mark's eyes opened wide as he suddenly realized what his wife was telling him. He began to say something, when he was interrupted by Maggie who cried, "Shut up and listen to me, for once, Mark. Ever since we were married, I've been trying to tell you something, but you never seem to want to hear anything I have to say. So, for once, could you please listen to me?"

Silently, Mark nodded his head and allowed his wife to speak.

Maggie went on to explain, "A few years ago, I had a child out of wedlock by Erik Masterson."

Mark's eyes were opened to Maggie's revelation about her drinking problem. He was amazed and a bit ashamed at how long she had been able to hide this problem from him, for so long. He cringed at the thought of how inattentive he really had been to her needs, and he also came to the realization of how difficult a position as the pastor's wife he had placed her in. It was a role that was fraught with all sorts of impossible expectations by him as well as by members of the congregation. For the first time since he had known her, Mark felt great compassion for his young wife. He began to feel for her. He began to fall in love with this woman all over again, for she was truly a remarkable woman for confessing to him all of these things. He smiled at his wife and he began to stroke her unruly hair, with his right hand, all along whispering, to her that all was forgiven. He told her that she need not be alone with her problems, that he loved her and truly cared for her, despite everything that she had just confessed.

Maggie swallowed hard, as she continued, "Mark! There's more. I have more to tell you."

Mark whispered, "Services are going to begin, soon, Maggie. Go and get cleaned up and we can talk later."

"No!" Maggie demanded. "I must tell you something else. It's something that I've been blocking from my memory. Ever since it happened, I've completely suppressed it."

Mark listened, once again, quietly, as Maggie continued, "I don't know how else to say this, Mark. I guess I'll just come right out and tell you. I was there the night Adam and Denise were killed."

Mark's eyes opened wide with delight, as he asked Maggie, "You were an eyewitness?

That's wonderful news. You know who caused the accident, then."

Maggie's eyes overflowed once again, as she nodded, "Yes, Mark, I know who killed Adam and Denise."

Mark asked, with excitement, "Who, then, Maggie? Who killed Adam and Denise?"

Maggie cried out, "I did, Mark! I killed Adam and Denise. I'm so sorry! I'm sorry, Mark! I'm so sorry."

Samantha asked Valerie how she was doing, while Erik attempted to help Alice stand up.

Valerie laughed a little uneasily, " It feels like I just had a baby."

Alice managed a laugh herself, as she said, "You feel like you just had a baby! I did just have a baby. So, what are we waiting for, people? Let's go."

"Go?" Erik asked. "Go where? I told you that your friend sped off in my car."

Alice walked, slowly, over toward Valerie and said, "If I can make it to that church of yours, maybe Jesus can perform another miracle. Maybe he can bring me back my baby."

Valerie shouted, "If you can make it to church, Woman, in your condition, well then, I can make it, too."

Samantha told Erik, "Call for a cab and then call your car phone to inform Rico where we'll be should he somehow catch up with that cop and the baby."

After doing so, Erik returned to the room to find Alice wearing a clean set of clothes that she had hanging in a closet.

"Our limo...I mean our taxi has arrived," Erik announced, proudly.

After everyone climbed into the cab, Samantha asked the taxi cab driver to let her off at her mother's house.

After leaving the cab, Samantha walked up to her mother's house. Before knocking at the door, she turned around and noticed a strange car parked in the street, directly in front of the house. A bad feeling came over Samantha, as she headed for the back door, which led into the kitchen.

Lincoln entered the church with his grandmother, who walked alongside him with her arm linked inside of his. They were greeted by several people, and when they reached the pew, where Peggy and Rosemary sat, Lincoln's grandmother paused to say hello.

"I'm so sorry to hear about your children, Ladies."

Rosemary whispered, "Thank you, MaryFaye!"

Peggy simply, continued to stare forward, with bloodshot eyes.

Lincoln ushered his grandmother forward, as they made their way toward the front of the church.

Valerie and Alice made their way, slowly, into the church. Chris turned around, instinctively, spotted Valerie, and then rushed to her side full of questions.

Valerie told Chris, "I'll tell you the whole story, later, Chris. But, for now, I've got to find a seat for my friend, Alice. She gave birth today. She shouldn't even be out of bed. We came here, this evening, praying for a miracle."

Chris smiled, as he helped Valerie find Alice a seat.

Pastor Mark appeared from the back of the church, located Lincoln, and whispered to him that there would be a slight delay in services tonight, that if he would please play something on his guitar in the meantime, it would be greatly appreciated.

Lincoln whispered to his grandmother that he was going to his car to retrieve his guitar.

While Lincoln was gone, an inspiration came to MaryFaye.

The intruder pointed his revolver toward Derek, as he said, "Someone wants you dead, Mr. Holmes. Someone wants you dead real bad. They're paying me two thousand dollars to off you, my friend. Isn't it nice to find out how much your life is worth right before you, die?"

Derek stuttered nervously, "Just...just don't......just......don't hur...... hurt my wife. She hasn't done anything. She's com......comple...... completely innocent."

"I was told that there was to be no witnesses, Mr. Holmes."

Helen glanced over toward her husband, as he valiantly attempted to grab the revolver from the intruder's hand. During the struggle a shot rang out, which ricocheted off of a wall behind Helen, narrowly missing her.

"That was close, Mr. Holmes," the intruder said as he grew angrier with each passing moment.

Derek pleaded, "Please let my wife go free. I promise she won't turn you in."

The intruder laughed, as he asked, "What good is the promise of a dead man, Mr. Holmes?"

Derek began to feel very helpless, as he realized that he and his wife were doomed.

As Lincoln made his way back into the church, he sat down on a chair in front of the congregation, and began to softly strum his guitar.

MaryFaye, with cane in hand, walked up to the front of the church and stood beside her grandson. She whispered something in his ear, which caused him to grin.

Derek pleaded once more that the life of his wife be spared, just as the intruder, again pointed the gun toward Helen.

"I figure it's like this," the intruder explained, "if I kill the little lady first, well, then you most likely won't have anything left to live for, Mr. Holmes. Thus, it'll be a piece of cake when it comes to be your turn. Then, my job is done."

Derek cringed, helplessly, as he watched the intruder pull back on the trigger of the revolver.

Derek shouted, "No!"

The intruder was taken back by surprise, when, as he pulled the trigger, a figure leaped into the room, blocking the bullet from reaching it's intended target.

Acting quickly, and taking full advantage of the gunman's dazed reaction, Derek managed to grab the revolver from his hands, causing the intruder to flee out of the house fearing for his own life.

MaryFaye began to sing, "As it was in the beginning, is now until the end. Woman draws her life from man and gives it back again. There is love. There is love. Man shall leave his mother and woman leave her home. They shall wander off to where the two shall be as one. There is love. There is love."

Tears began to flow down Rosemary's cheeks, uncontrollably, for Peggy was to sing that very song at Adam and Denise's wedding. She recalled like it were just yesterday, when Peggy practiced it in front of her.

Valerie made her way over to Peggy's side, and rubbed her gently on the arm. Peggy stood up, smiled peacefully down at Valerie, and then made her way up front. As she stood beside MaryFaye, Peggy placed her arm around the older woman, kissed her gently on the cheek, and then she joined in the singing.

Everyone stood up as the two women continued to sing. At the conclusion of the song, Lincoln started up another tune. When the two women recognized the melody they chimed in with Lincoln's strumming.

While everyone sang along to the tune, "Beautiful Savior," Alice made her way up front with tears flowing down her cheeks.

Valerie joined Alice as she knelt down at the altar to pray. Valerie, gently massaged Alice's back, while she prayed silently.

Julia began to cry, as she remembered all of the emotions she felt when she accepted Christ earlier that morning.

Chris took Julia by the hand and smiled.

Outside of the church some late arrivals were getting out of their cars. Scott walked up to Helen and Derek, and held out his hand.

"Hello, Mr. and Mrs. Holmes! Is Samantha already here?"

Helen shook her head, slowly, with a tear stained face, she announced, solemnly, "Samantha went to be with our Lord Jesus Christ, today, Scott."

Scott's eyes immediately filled with tears, for he was beginning to realize that his feelings for Samantha had grown much more deeper than a friendship. He had been asking God if Samantha was his intended. Now, he realized, it was too late for him and Samantha. Somehow, he came to realize time had just slipped away.

Suddenly, Rico drove up into the church lot and, quickly parked his car next to Scott's.

Derek, Helen and Scott watched as Rico rushed past them into the church.

Derek turned toward his wife and asked her, "What was that in his arms?"

Helen replied, "I think I know, but I'm not sure. It was so tiny."

A hush fell over the church as Rico rushed in, looking around, frantically. Valerie stood up and spotted the young man, smiled and waved him forward, as she said to Alice, "God is truly an awesome God, Alice."

As Alice slowly stood up, and turned around to face Rico, her tears of pain, suddenly turned to tears of joy, as she shouted praises, "Thank you, Jesus! Thank you, Jesus!"

Rico handed the baby boy over to Alice and remarked, "You know what, Alice? I swear he's got my nose."

Alice thought for a minute and then she wrapped her free arm around Rico's neck and cried, "I think he does, too, now that I think about it. Oh, Rico, our son is so beautiful. Thank you, Jesus. Praise you, Jesus."

Lincoln began to play another tune on his guitar. Soon, everyone recognized it to be, "Victory in Jesus."

There wasn't a dry eye in the entire church, as everyone sang along with MaryFaye and Peggy.

Another hush fell upon the church, as Scott, Derek and Helen entered. Helen was crying softly, for the shock of watching her daughter die in her arms, was replaying over and over in her mind.

Valerie rushed over to Helen's side, and asked her, "Where is Samantha, Helen?"

Helen buried her head into her husband's chest, while, Scott stepped forward.

"What is it, Scott?" Valerie's voice began to tremble.

Scott slowly shook his head, while, solemnly looking downward.

Valerie cried out, "No! Not Samantha!"

Chris rushed to Valerie's side and allowed her to bury her head into his chest, while he stroked her long auburn hair.

Suddenly, Pastor Mark entered the room, with Maggie at his side. He was helping to keep Maggie from falling completely apart, as they made their way up to the front.

Mark thanked Lincoln, who picked up the guitar and then ushered the women back to their seats.

After everyone was seated, Pastor Mark turned his own red, bloodshot eyes toward the congregation while he held his trembling wife up.

"Brothers and Sisters," he began, "my wife and I have something to tell you. It's something that was brought to my attention only moments ago. It seems the mystery surrounding the hit and run accident that claimed the lives of Adam Harrison and Denise Washington has just been solved."

Rosemary and Peggy turned to one another with surprise at their Pastor's words.

Pastor Mark continued, "I, regretfully, must take my share of the blame for the accident that took the lives of two much beloved members of our Christian family. It was my ignorance and my failure to see just what exactly my wife was going through, which eventually led to the premature demise of Adam and Denise. I was unaware of the problems with which my dear wife was dealing. I failed to be attentive to her needs, as she struggled to deal with the prestige and responsibilities associated with being a Pastor's wife. As it turns out, my wife had been struggling with things from her past, that she couldn't find a way of escaping from. She turned to a secret lifestyle unbecoming a Pastor's wife. She developed a crutch. Her crutch was leaning on a man made substance, instead of leaning on our Savior, Jesus Christ. That was her first and foremost mistake. I mean, that was our mistake. Like I said, earlier, I share in the blame. My wife had been leaning on that substance instead of being in constant prayer, to deal with her problems, on that fateful night, when Adam and Denise left this world."

Pastor Mark cleared his throat, caught his breath, and continued, "My wife had blocked this memory from her mind, until today, when it came flooding back to her. I pray that each and everyone of you can find it in your hearts to forgive my wife and myself, as I reveal to you, that it was Maggie who was the driver of that other car, which forced Adam to strike that tree, which killed him and his fiancee'. If you cannot forgive us, I will understand, and I will not blame you, nor judge you. I can't even imagine what it would be like to be out there in your shoes, as I offer up my resignation, as we report this information to the proper authorities. All that I ask you, is for your prayers, as my wife must pay for her crime. No matter what your decision is, I will always stand by my wife. No matter what. Thank you. May God bless you all. I pray that you reach your decision with an open mind and loving heart. We will be waiting in my office while you deliberate. Thank you."

As Mark and Maggie made their way to the rear of the church, Lincoln made his way to the front of the room with his guitar. He began to play,"Amazing Grace."

Mark stopped midway, and turned back to face his congregation, as they sang along with Lincoln.

Mark turned his head toward his wife, and found her crying tears of mixed emotions. For the first time, since he had met her, he sensed that the possibility of inner peace might be starting to grow.

Mark mingled through the congregation and thanked each and everyone for their loving and kind, forgiving hearts.

Maggie attempted to shrink away, against the wall, but was stopped, suddenly, when Peggy Washington came face to face with her. The sadness and despair in Peggy's eyes were more than Maggie could withstand. Maggie began to cry tears of self torment, while Peggy stood there, staring down at her, without saying a word.

Suddenly, Peggy wrapped her arms around Maggie, filling her so full of God's warm love and forgiveness.

After everyone settled back in their seats, Pastor Mark returned to his pulpit. He offered up praise to the Lord. He went on to explain that the Holy spirit was truly alive and well, and was most assuredly in their very presence this evening.

After several shouts of praises were spoken by various members of the congregation, Pastor Mark said, "And now it is time to make you all an offer. This offer comes directly from our Lord Jesus Christ. He suffered on this earth, at the hands of the very people he was sent down here by his Heavenly Father, to save from eternal Hell. Our Lord simply asks you to confess your sins to him. Allow him to enter your heart. Allow him to become your Lord and personal Savior. You need to give our Lord all of your cares and needs. Allow him to take over from here. We can't live without Jesus. Our lives can become so messed up when we try to live the way we want to, instead of the righteous way. God's way. So, if you feel the Holy Spirit dealing with you, tonight, well then, don't fight it. Come forward. We never know when it will be too late."

Lincoln came forward and began to play, "Just As I Am," on his guitar. The congregation began to sing softly.

Julia looked over toward Chris and smiled, while Alice took Rico by the hand and together, they knelt down at the altar, and prayed, silently.

Maggie walked slowly to the front of the church, praising God the whole way, as she finally decided to give it all over to Jesus. She finally decided to stop playing the role of a Christian, as she knelt down beside Alice and her baby to make peace with her Savior.

Helen looked questioningly over toward her husband, who finally let go of her arm, as he, suddenly, no longer felt capable of restraining her from going forward.

As Helen walked forward, she felt her daughter's spirit walking with her arm in arm. Helen smiled proudly at the people who were watching her, as she made her way to the altar. She didn't feel a bit ashamed for she was answering her daughter's greatest prayer.

A miracle was truly happening, tonight

CHAPTER FOUR

RECTIFICATION

Several days later, Samantha Taylor's lifeless body lay in an open coffin at the Greene-Manville Funeral Home. Helen sat quietly in a chair. Derek stood in a nearby corner, struggling nervously against his urge to light up a cigarette.

A hand rested upon Helen's shoulder, unexpectedly. Helen turned to find Valerie Rhodes, who was attempting to develop some sort of calm about herself.

"Thank you for coming, Valerie," Helen cried. "Samantha adored you so much."

Valerie's eyes filled with moisture, uncontrollably, as she whispered, "Samantha was incredible, Helen."

Helen glanced over toward the open casket which held her only child and nodded, proudly, in silent agreement.

Maggie sat in a small jail cell, awaiting the fate that was going to be handed down to her. She had spoken to her lawyer, and after quiet prayer and meditation, she had decided to waive her right to a trial. After admitting her guilt before Judge Youngblood, Maggie had written a letter explaining exactly how she felt about the crime she had committed.

Maggie read the letter before the judge in his chambers. The witnesses had included her husband Mark, the prosecutor, her own lawyer, along with Peggy Washington and Rosemary Harrison.

Trembling slightly, Maggie had begun to read aloud to the assembled group, "I, Maggie Jensen, do solemnly swear that the contents of this letter are the whole truth and nothing but the whole truth. I stand before Your Honor and my almighty Redeemer with a heavy burden of guilt weighing down upon my shoulders. I, would first, like to emphasize the reason why it has taken me so long to come forth with my admission of guilt. The reason, to put it simply, was because of the mere fact that I had blocked this terrible crime completely from my mind. It wasn't until I was placed in a situation of tremendous emotional stress, that this horrible memory came flooding back to me like a torrential rainstorm. When this memory was revealed to me I immediately went to my husband and confessed everything to him.

"I have since dealt with the pain and torment of my guilt for taking the lives of two very dear friends, who were both loved and adored by our entire congregation. I have dealt with the reality that I am an alcoholic, who turns to the bottle when under pressure instead of turning to our precious Lord Jesus Christ.

"It may sound strange to everyone, that of all people, the wife of the pastor would resort to such an evil and corrupt method of coping with everyday life, such as consuming alcohol.

"But, as everyone has no doubt by now realized, I am merely human just like everyone else in this room.

"I am by no means placing this burden of guilt upon anyone but myself. I have spoken to my Savior Jesus Christ, and I have asked him for his forgiveness. I have received the blessings of his kindness, and I have felt the warmth of his forgiveness. I am no longer troubled about my sin, however, I shall have to live with the reality of what I have done. I am by no means whatsoever letting myself off the hook. I must live with the memory of my crime for the remainder of my life.

"I am sincerely remorseful for what I have done, and I do not wish the court to extend any sort of leniency on my behalf. The good Lord will judge me in the end for my actions. I only pray that he will show me mercy.

"I am fully prepared to allow the court to pass judgment upon myself. I would like, however, to explain to the families of my victims that this nightmare was totally involuntary. It was as if I were demon possessed when I perpetrated this horrendous deed.

"I realize the dangers that consuming alcohol can present in someone's life. It just completely changes their personality and opens up so many avenues for evil to enter into.

"I am truly sorry for my actions, and I am prepared to hear my punishment. Maggie Jensen."

Shaun Collins lay in his own bed, glancing out toward his bedroom window, as the noon day sun shone brightly through his thin, yellow curtains. Shaun winced at the pain that he was feeling. The pain was a result of the latest beating that he had endured at the hands of two thugs, who had attempted to rob him, the night when Rico had discovered him lying behind a dumpster.

Shaun, now regretted trying to walk on his badly bruised legs. He was also quite conscious of the gruesome sight of that young man who had taken his own life with a gun. It was a memory that was deeply embedded into Shaun's mind. Shaun was beginning to look at this memory as a sort of wake up call for himself and he was just realizing how precious and dear life truly was, and just how fragile a person can become.

Although Shaun realized that he had never ever entertained the thought of taking his own life, he, however, realized that he was constantly putting himself into dangerous situations, that could, in themselves, be construed as being quite irrational and detrimental to his own well being.

Shaun also realized that Scott and Valerie possessed something very wonderful. He was not sure what it was, but he so desperately wanted to discover it.

Shaun's thoughts were abruptly disturbed when he realized that he was not alone in his room.

Lingering in a dark corner was a huge burly man. He was smoking a foul smelling cigar. Shaun squinted his eyes to make out the man's features. He must have been one of his mother's latest boyfriends. He was not looking forward to being introduced. Given the track record of his mother, he knew it was a sick and depraved choice.

MaryFaye MacWilliams began to pour herself a cup of hot tea, while the warmth of the Autumn sun shone through her kitchen windows.

After placing the teapot back upon the stove, MaryFaye stepped over toward the counter to retrieve the morning newspaper. About midway toward the counter, MaryFaye was forced to stop in her tracks, for she had suddenly felt a sharp pain. Clutching her chest tightly, MaryFaye's eyes were filled with pain and agony.

Whispering, softly, MaryFaye began to pray, "Lord, please help me. I plead with you, Dear Lord. I am not, yet, ready to leave this world. There is so much for me to do. If it is your will to take me from this earth, well then, I'll go willingly. But, please Lord, there is still something I must do. You know what it is, Lord. Please guide me along the path that will lead me there. It is your will that must be done and not my own. Please cleanse my heart and give me a renewed spirit. Show me who it is that you wish for me to help, and then dear precious Jesus, I will join you in Heaven."

As Peggy Washington and Rosemary Harrison entered the funeral parlor, arm in arm, they were greeted by Scott, who looked as if he had not gotten any sleep in weeks.

"Thank you for coming, Ladies. Helen and Derek are talking to Valerie over there in the corner."

Peggy glanced over toward the corner that Scott had indicated, and then she whispered, "How is Helen holding up?"

Scott replied, "Quite well, actually. She is every bit as remarkable as Samantha."

As Peggy and Rosemary made their way into the room, they were followed in by Erik Masterson, who was dressed in a black silk tux, with a starched white shirt.

Scott extended his hand toward Erik and said, "I'm glad that you could make it, Erik. Helen will be pleased to see you. She may need all of the comfort that she can get before this day is through."

Erik shook Scott's hand and nodded, in silent agreement, as he fought back the tears that were beginning to form in his eyes.

Scott noticed Erik's tears, and he too, found himself fighting back tears of his own.

After Scott retreated to an empty corner of the room, he knelt down to pray silently.

Valerie glanced over toward Scott and instinctively knew not to disturb him, so she excused herself away from Derek and Helen. She took Scott's place at the door as she noticed that more people were beginning to mingle in, slowly.

"Alice! Rico!" Valerie squealed softly. "I'm so glad that you were able to come."

Alice handed over a small bundle, wrapped in a pale blue blanket to Valerie, who squealed a bit louder, this time.

"Oh, he's so precious, Alice," Valerie cried, while Rico beamed with pride.

"He's a chip off the old block!" Rico laughed.

Alice giggled, "Rico, I didn't realize that you were into old worn out expressions."

Rico's face reddened, slightly, as he said, "I guess it comes with the territory, Alice. You know, fatherhood and everything. I guess pretty soon I'll be wearing my old man's tweed suits and clip on ties."

Valerie laughed, and remarked, "Somehow, I don't think so, Rico."

Chris and Julia sat outside on the steps of the funeral parlor, hesitating, before deciding to go on in.

"It was not your fault, Chris," Julia explained. "You could not have stopped Lucas from shooting himself, even if you had been given a chance to try."

Chris' eyes filled with tears, as he whispered, hoarsely, "I may not have had the chance to talk him out of it, Julia, but I had been given the chance to tell him about Jesus.....about how much he was loved by Jesus. That's where I failed Lucas."

Julia, who's eyes were completely dry, and who was keeping everything under complete control, placed her arm around Chris' shoulders while stroking his hair with her other hand.

"Chris," Julia spoke in a very warm and compassionate tone. "You cannot continue to beat yourself up over this. Lucas is gone and there is nothing we can do to bring him back to us. No one loved him more than we did, Chris. Not even his own family."

"No, Julia," Chris said, as he wiped away at the moisture that was forming around his flaring nostrils. "I didn't love him like you did. If

I had, then I wouldn't have abandoned him these past two years, like I did. At least he was fortunate to have you in his life."

Julia took Chris' face in her hands and said to him, while forcing him to look her straight in the eyes, "Look here, Chris, you found something that Lucas hadn't found. You found your Lord and personal Savior. You did what you thought was right. You avoided Lucas because you knew that Jesus didn't approve of his lifestyle, and you didn't want to become embroiled in all of that again. Jesus delivered you from the pits of despair. If he hadn't, you could very well have ended up precisely in the same way that Lucas ended up."

Chris' eyes were filled to the brim with tears, that suddenly overflowed and ran down his cheeks, as he hugged Julia tightly.

Still crying, Chris said, "I wish that I could have turned his life around for him. I wish that I could have been there for him. It all hurts so much."

MaryFaye sat down on an overstuffed sofa and let out a deep breath. She held her eyes shut as she felt the pain in her chest subside, slightly. She repeated over and over again, "Thank you Jesus. Thank you sweet Jesus. Glory be your name, Jesus."

Lincoln walked over toward Helen with his guitar in hand. He leaned down and allowed her to whisper something in his ear. Afterward, Lincoln nodded with a smile. As everyone gathered in their seats, Lincoln stood in front of the crowd, glanced over toward Samantha and then he began to strum softly upon his guitar. As he played softly, he began to speak.

Lincoln's voice was quite soothing and calm, as was the music that he was playing.

"Friends, we are not gathered here to mourn the passing of our dear sister Samantha. We are, however, here to celebrate her life. Her life, which was full of so many good things. Our dear beloved Samantha, as we all knew, was a very kind and charitable soul. She never had an unkind word to say about anyone. Instead, when she was placed with disagreeable people or uncomfortable situations, she was always the first to suggest that we pray about this person, or she would say, 'Let's take it to the Lord.'

"She had incredible strength. I'm not talking about physical strength, you know. I'm referring to the incredible strength that our Lord Jesus Christ had bestowed upon her. She overcame so many spiritual roadblocks in her life. Through her unwavering faith in our Lord, Samantha overcame the trauma of watching her own father blow his head off right before her eyes at the tender age of eight. Our good Lord helped her get through that. There were several times that Samantha had told me about when she felt that Satan was trying to combat her in spiritual warfare. She informed me that the more Satan tried his little tricks on her, the stronger she became, for she found herself reaching out to our Lord during these times and asking him for his guidance and protection. Samantha was like an angel in our lives. She was always the one who was the first to be there when asked for help. She never hesitated and she never regretted going out of her way when it came to a friend in need. I remember one time, a few years back, when I called upon Samantha to help me when my car was stolen out of the parking lot at a restaurant. Samantha came to my aid immediately, dropping everything that she was doing, and together we took it upon ourselves to rely upon our faith in our Lord Jesus Christ. We sat in her car, and we prayed to the good Lord for the perpetrators to have a change of heart and return my car, no questions asked. I must say it was Samantha's faith that returned my car to me. Because, I can tell you right here and now, I was thinking at the time that there was no way in, you know where, that my car was ever going to be seen again. At least not in the same condition it was in when it had been taken from me.

"Well, to make a long story......less long, after we finished praying, Samantha looked off in the direction that the young kids had gone in. After several minutes passed by, I was ready to get the police involved, but Samantha insisted we wait and be patient. She told me that my car was going to be back momentarily, and that the good Lord had changed those young car thieves from the inside out.

"Lo and behold, just as Samantha had said, my car came rolling up slowly into the parking lot. As I walked over to the two young kids to get my keys back, the driver was shaking a bit. I helped him out of the car and he immediately began to cry to me, an apology, saying, 'I've never done anything like this before, Mister. Please don't turn me in. I'm really sorry.'

"Well, Samantha came right up to those boys and told them about the Lord's forgiveness for our sins. Those two boys were so receptive of Samantha's testimony that they both got down on their knees, immediately, and accepted Christ. They even attended our church a couple of times. And to make this story even more incredible, those same two boys went off to seminary school. It truly is awesome what God can do through us."

Everyone clapped their hands softly in celebration of Jesus' unending mercy.

Shaun spoke to the figure lurking in the dark, "Who are you?"

"Your guardian angel, Kid," the man answered, sarcastically. "You better not try to talk, your mother doesn't want you to overdo it."

"My mother," Shaun whispered. "Where is my mother?"

"Margie ran down to the store to pick some things up. She's asked me to baby-sit you."

Shaun sneered, "I don't need a baby-sitter."

"I know that, Kid," the man agreed. "But....ah....let's humor your mother some, Kid. She's trying to develop some maternal hormones, I think."

Shaun grinned with a great deal of effort, as he repeated, "Maternal hormones."

"Yeah," the man spoke through the smoky haze, "earlier, she was blubbering about never being a good mother to you, or something."

Shaun cried out, "She doesn't have to feel guilty about what happened to me."

"No, Kid," the man said as he exhaled another puff of foul smelling smoke. "You're not following me. She doesn't feel like she caused you to get hurt, but she does feel like she failed you by not giving you a proper role model in your puny short life. I swear, kids nowadays, mess up their lives and immediately they start blaming their parents. It's always the parents' fault. Kids, nowadays, never take on the blame themselves for screwing up their own lives. They are always using their parents as scape goats."

Shaun rolled his eyes as he listened to his mother's latest boyfriend's ever enlightening philosophy.

Lincoln stopped strumming his guitar and he asked Helen, "What was Samantha's favorite hymn?"

Helen smiled and announced proudly, "The Old Rugged Cross! Samantha was always singing it around the house. She had a beautiful voice."

Lincoln asked Scott, Chris and Valerie to join him up front.

After they were all assembled, Lincoln announced, "A few short days before Samantha went to be with our precious Savior, the five of us formed an alliance. We are now down to four. Our mission was and is to spread the gospel of our dear Lord Jesus Christ, everywhere we go. Samantha will truly be missed by our new found alliance, but the four of us remaining shall persevere for Jesus' sake. And now......"

As Lincoln strummed the music to Samantha's favorite hymn, he and the other three began to sing the hymn which was so lovingly dedicated to their fallen sister in Christ.

The morning following Samantha's burial service, found Lincoln walking up the steps of Valerie's apartment building. He found Valerie looking through her mail in the corridor.

"Oh! Hi there, Lincoln," Valerie greeted her friend with a warm hug.

"I hope their not all bills, Val," Lincoln laughed.

"No, actually, only one of them has the distinction of being a bill."

"Oh," Lincoln commented, "that's good."

After seeing the troubled look upon her face, Lincoln asked, "Isn't it good, Val?"

"I don't know," Valerie said with a very furrowed forehead.

"What is it, Val?" Lincoln asked not out of curiosity but more out of genuine concern.

"It......it's a letter from my father," Valerie explained.

"Your father?"

"Yes," Valerie replied, sounding a bit bewildered.

"Maybe it's good news, Val," Lincoln suggested as Valerie tore into the envelope.

"When is the last time that you've seen him or heard from him, Val?" Lincoln asked.

"It's been over eight years, Lincoln."

Lincoln let out a whistle and then he watched Valerie as she read the letter, silently, in a corner of the corridor.

Shaun awoke that morning to find himself alone in his room, which pleased him just fine. He reached over to the side of his bed and found a set of crutches. He listened for a few minutes in order to determine whether or not anyone was awake in the house. After he was convinced that no one was stirring about, he threw his covers aside and he began to struggle out of bed.

Successfully placing his feet upon the wooden floor, Shaun then attempted to maneuver the crutches underneath his arms. Initially, Shaun appeared to be a bit unstable on the crutches as he tried to stand. Twice, Shaun's weakened legs almost gave out beneath him.

Perseverance, however, paid off, as Shaun practiced walking around his room, slowly regaining confidence in his badly bruised legs.

"And now," Shaun whispered, "for the real test."

Shaun took in a deep breath, let it out slowly, and then he started to walk out of his bedroom, toward the kitchen.

As he struggled to open his bedroom door, Shaun froze dead in his tracks. He found his mother's latest boyfriend standing outside his door, with his two burly arms crossed in front of him, grinning like a crazed lunatic.

Chris was hard at work that same morning, grateful to be busy. He was trying not to concentrate upon the deaths of his two friends, Lucas and Samantha.

After successfully completing his latest assignment, Chris wandered over to the vending machine for his first break of the morning. While standing there in front of the machine, Chris suddenly noticed his own reflection in the window. A voice from somewhere deep inside of himself seemed to be calling out to him, as he stared at his own reflection.

Chris noticed worry lines forming across his forehead as well as the dark bags that were beginning to form underneath his eyes, due to a lack of proper sleep.

Chris' expression made a turn for the worse when he began to hear deeply embedded thoughts come rushing to the surface, from the inner depths of his subconscious.

Chris felt his eyes begin to water up, totally unexpectedly, when he heard a voice from within say, "How could you let Lucas down like that, Johnson? He was reaching out to you and you just let him slip away."

Chris swiped away at the tears that were falling down his face, as he struggled to make his reflection disappear so he could make a selection from the vending machine. However, his reflection was becoming more and more clear to him, as the voice returned, saying, "You let Lucas down in the worst way, and now he's gone. He's gone forever and there is nothing that you or anyone else can do to bring him back. You should have helped him when you had the chance, instead you helped yourself to Julia."

Chris shouted, "No!"

As he regained control upon reality, Chris quickly glanced around to find a couple of female coworkers approaching him. One of the girls, who's name had temporarily escaped Chris, walked up behind him, placed an arm around his shoulders, and whispered, "Chris, everything will get better in time."

MaryFaye walked over to the huge bay window in her living room and peered through her pale blue curtains. She smiled as she watched two squirrels playing around her huge oak tree out in her front yard.

"Looks like fun, little ones," MaryFaye said with a smile.

Just as she was about to sit down in her rocking chair, MaryFaye heard the doorbell. The bell sounded one more time, before she reached the door. She opened the door to find her young neighbor standing outside on the porch.

"Hi there, neighbor," the young woman greeted MaryFaye, joyfully.

"Marissa, girl," MaryFaye shouted. "When did you get back from Europe?"

"Late last night, Mrs. MacWilliams," Marissa a small, thin woman of about twenty years, informed the older woman.

"Come on in, Girl," MaryFaye begged, stepping aside so as to allow the woman to enter, as she added, "Would you care for some tea?"

Marissa replied, "Oh, no. Don't go to any bother. I just wanted to see how you were doing, that's all."

MaryFaye closed the screen door, and motioned for Marissa to find a seat.

"Oh, these old bones aren't getting any stronger, you know, Dear," MaryFaye answered, with a sigh, as she made her way over to the rocking chair.

"You need someone to come over here to help you and care for you, every now and then."

MaryFaye sat down and let out her breath, and nodded, as she said, "I think that my grandson will be coming around more often, now, Marissa."

Marissa's eyebrows lifted with mild expectation, as she inquired, "Are you referring to Lincoln?"

MaryFaye nodded while grinning broadly toward Marissa.

Suddenly, Marissa started to fidget around, nervously, in her chair.

MaryFaye laughed, "You kind of got a thing for my grandson, haven't you, Child?"

Marissa's eyes suddenly could not look directly into MaryFaye's as she began to look elsewhere in the room.

"What's the letter say, Valerie? If you don't mind my asking, that is."

Valerie placed the letter in her pocket and looked around the corridor absentmindedly.

She began to ascend the stairs toward her apartment, with Lincoln following behind her closely.

Rubbing Valerie's elbow gently as she unlocked her door, Lincoln followed her inside.

After the door was closed, Valerie wrapped her arms around Lincoln's neck.

Valerie whispered, "Hold me, Lincoln. Please, just hold me for awhile."

Lincoln obliged his friend. He closed his eyes as he felt her trembling against his body.

Scott stood in front of Samantha's newly dug grave and placed some fresh flowers at her tombstone. He, then, stood back, and folded his hands in front, while he whispered softly, "Hey there, Samantha! What's it like up there? I bet you're sitting up there in the presence of God, having the time of your life......"

Scott grinned, "The time of your life......."

As several birds began to chirp, merrily, nearby, Scott looked up toward the beautiful blue skies. As he was drinking in God's splendor, a hand upon his shoulder, caused him to jump a bit.

As he turned around, Scott exclaimed, "Erik! Are you still here? I thought that you would be returning to California by now."

Erik, holding a small bouquet of flowers himself, replied, "I'll be leaving in a couple of days, Scott."

Scott nodded and then he returned his gaze toward Samantha's tombstone.

"You were in love with her, weren't you, Scott?" Erik asked, as he watched Scott's concentration.

Scott shrugged his shoulders and replied, "In my own way, I suppose, I was, Erik. But I wasn't aware of it, until it was too late. Sometimes you don't realize what you have until you lose it."

Erik placed the flowers that he had brought, down next to Scott's flowers. As he stood back up, Erik agreed, "You're right, my man. You are so right. Samantha was so easy to love. I was a fool to break off my engagement to her."

Scott looked straight at Erik and asked, "Why did you break it off with Samantha?"

Erik replied, "It's very, very complicated, my friend."

Scott motioned for Erik to join him over toward a small bench that stood nearby, as he asked, "Erik, what, exactly, are your plans, now?"

Erik sat beside Scott and replied while scratching his head, "I'm not sure. For one thing, before I go back to California, I'm going to visit Maggie in jail."

Scott's face turned to an expression of confusion, as he asked, "Maggie? Why on earth would you visit Maggie before you return home?"

"Scott," Erik explained, "it's a long story, but Maggie and I have a history."

Scott glanced over toward Samantha's grave, surveyed the foliage, and then he turned back toward Erik, who was now facing the ground that lay out before him.

Maggie stirred in her cot, which was extremely uncomfortable, as she slowly awoke from a dream. She struggled to remember this dream, but found that it had somehow escaped her. The only thing she could figure out, was that it had something to do with Tyler, her son. A noise coming from the cell beside hers, brought Maggie to her feet. She was dressed in prison blue and her hair was extremely unkempt. Her mouth felt very dry, and her breath, she felt, was quite certainly foul, as she stepped to the front of her cell.

"Guard?" Maggie called out.

A dark skinned, burly prison guard stepped out of the shadows and asked in a rough voice, "What is it, Princess?"

Maggie tried to smile, but was extremely conscious of the condition her mouth was in, so she merely smiled with her mouth closed.

"Well, spit it out, Your Highness," the guard demanded. "What can I do for you?"

Maggie replied, "I must speak to someone."

The guard replied, "Your husband will be here this afternoon, Lady Guinevere. He hasn't missed a day yet."

"No!" Maggie exclaimed. "Not my husband. I must speak to a friend of mine."

"You're allowed a phone call, Your Majesty. If there is someone on the outside that you wish to contact, you can call him on the phone."

"I don't know his number, Goldie," Maggie explained. "He's just visiting."

"I'm sorry, Mademoiselle," the guard laughed. "I can't help you."

After the guard disappeared down the hallway, Maggie sat down on her cot, stared at the four blank walls, buried her face into her hands and began to weep, silently.

"Get back in bed, Kid!"

Shaun almost fell, as the man's thunderous voice completely startled him.

"Tell my mother that I need to see her, Bluto!" Shaun demanded, bravely.

The man's face turned beet red as he screamed, "My name's not Bluto, Kid. You watch too many Popeye cartoons."

Shaun repeated, louder this time, "I need to see my mother, Mister. Where is she?"

A door down the hall opened, suddenly, and Shaun watched as his mother came flying down the hallway toward him. Her nightgown was flying around her long slender legs.

"Shaun, dear," Margie called out in a scratchy voice, "what do you want, Baby?"

Shaun grinned defiantly toward the huge man who was still standing before him trying to look intimidating.

"I need to talk to you, Mother," Shaun explained.

After glancing toward the man, Shaun added, "Privately, that is."

The man stared down Margie, as if he were expecting her to take sides, and then he gave Shaun a look as if he wanted, in the worst way, to murder him in his sleep.

The man reluctantly grabbed his thin jacket, and hat as he left the house, slamming the door on his way out.

"You really should give him a chance, Shaun," the thin woman pleaded, while she helped Shaun into the kitchen.

After they reached the table, Shaun attempted to sit himself down. After a few failed attempts, he gave up and allowed his mother to help him.

"Are your ribs still sore. Honey?" she asked, while placing his crutches in a corner.

"Yes, Mother," he answered. "They're still pretty sore."

"What can I do for you, Baby?" she began to cry. "How can I make it better for you, Baby?"

"For starters," Shaun began, as he decided to seize the moment. "You can stop dating losers, Mother."

Shaun's mother shook her head, helplessly, as she said, "I wasn't referring to my social life, Dear. You can't control me like that. I can see whoever or whomever I please."

"Then," Shaun said while he stared directly into his mother's deep blue eyes, "I don't know how else to suggest to you how to make things better for me."

Margie's tears continued to fall down her face as she asked, "Can't I get you something for the pain, Shaun?"

"How about a gun, Mother?"

Margie's tears flowed more rapidly, as she cried, "Oh, no you don't, Buster! You're not doing that to me. I'm not going to clean your bloody carcass off of my nice clean carpets, just because you're going through some sort of adolescent emotional turmoil in your life. You're not doing that to me, Buddy."

Shaun half grinned, as he sarcastically laughed, "You're all heart, Mother."

Margie stood up, headed for the doorway, and then turned around and suggested, "You had better get a grip, Young Man, and stop feeling sorry for yourself."

Shaun watched his mother leave the room.

After his mother left, Shaun whispered, "You had better get a clue, Mother."

Erik headed straight for the jail house after leaving Scott standing in the cemetery. Outside of the prison, Erik bumped into Pastor Mark who had just arrived for his daily visit to Maggie.

"Pastor Mark," Erik extended his hand, uncertainly towards Mark, who was climbing out of his station wagon.

"Erik!" Mark exclaimed. "What on earth are you doing here? Did my wife send for you!"

Erik and Mark shook hands cordially, and they both walked towards the entrance of the prison, Erik explained, "As a matter of fact, she didn't send for me, Mark. I came here out of concern for her well being. I thought, perhaps, there might be something that I could do for her."

"Well," Pastor Mark, warned, "I hope that you won't upset her anymore than need be, Erik. As you know she's in a very fragile state of mind."

Erik nodded his head in contemplation, as the two men ascended the steps, and replied, "I realize that, Mark. I'm only here because Maggie might want me to be. I will do anything to help her."

Mark grinned, patted Erik on the back and said, "God bless you, Erik."

Alice laid her baby in his crib, and walked over toward Rico. She whispered in his ear, "Rico, we've got to discuss something, Baby."

Rico looked up from his motorcycle magazine, and then moved over to allow Alice to sit beside him on the sofa.

"What is it, Alice?" Rico asked. "If it's about me getting a job, I told you that I have a few possibilities I'm working on."

Alice sat beside Rico, and ran her hand up and down his right arm, and then she whispered, "No, it's not about your getting a job, Rico. I want to ask you if you felt anything the other day when we were kneeling down at the altar? You know, the day you rescued our baby from Mortie."

Rico looked straight forward, picturing that day in his mind, and then he turned toward Alice. He began to stroke her long hair. Smiling proudly, he said, "I did pretty good that day, didn't I, Babe?"

Alice smiled warmly at the sound of Rico's laughter and then she turned serious once again, as she asked him, "Did you accept Jesus Christ as your Lord and personal Savior like I did, that night, Rico?"

Rico shrugged as he explained, "I don't know nothing about accepting this Jesus Christ or anything, Alice, but I tell you what, I did feel the presence of something that night. I first felt it as I was chasing after that loser cop. I felt as if some higher power was helping me. I don't feel like I could have done that all by myself, you know."

Alice suddenly felt the presence of the Holy Spirit begin to fill the room, as they continued to discuss the events leading up to that night when she found salvation.

Alice whispered, "Tell me more, Rico. Tell me what you felt when we knelt down at the altar with our baby."

Rico thought about the question for another minute and then he replied, "I remember feeling that same presence, that thing I felt when I went after our son."

Alice decided to be blunt, "Rico, what I'm trying to find out is, did you accept Jesus Christ like I did?"

Rico slowly shook his head and answered, "No, Alice. I remember thanking God for helping me. I remember feeling so in awe of the miracle of our son. I was still reeling about figuring out that this baby was actually mine and not that dirt bag's."

Alice placed her head upon Rico's shoulder and smiled, as she said, "Rico, let's go back to church this Sunday. There's a message that I want you to hear. I know a way that we can be happy for the rest of our lives. In fact, I know a way that we can be happy for all eternity."

Maggie waited behind the cubicle for her first visitor of the day to appear opposite her. It turned out to be her husband.

"Mark," Maggie cried out softly, "it's so miserable in here. I think that I may very well lose my mind."

Mark's hands reached underneath the glass partition, and wrapped around Maggie's trembling hands.

"Hang in there, Darling! The entire congregation is praying for you."

Maggie's bloodshot eyes looked as if they hadn't been closed for days.

"I'm trying to be strong, Mark. I really am, but all I do is think about what I've done. I sit here and think about those two wonderful people I killed. When I think about how they were just starting their lives together and I came along and just snuffed their lives out like two candles in a storm."

Mark squeezed his wife's hands tighter and spoke to her soothingly, "Peggy and Rosemary have found it in their hearts to forgive you, Maggie. The good Lord, if you will only ask him to, will, also, forgive you. You've got to find some place in your own heart to forgive yourself. If you don't forgive yourself, then you will never find that inner peace that you so desperately need to find."

Maggie's tears began to flow down her cheeks, uncontrollably, as she dabbed at her nose with a handkerchief.

"Come on now, Maggie," Mark urged, "I think it's time that we pray about this."

Maggie wiped her face relatively dry and then she nodded in agreement. She admitted, "You're right, Mark. I already came to terms with my Maker, on the night we confessed everything before the congregation. I asked him to come into my life and take over from here.

I truly asked him to come into my heart that night and cleanse me. He really did, Mark, but now I'm suffering from tremendous guilt."

Mark held Maggie's hands, and said, softly, "Shhh....Maggie...,,Let's pray...."

Maggie bowed her head and closed her eyes as she prayed silently while her husband prayed aloud, "Dear Heavenly Father. I call upon you, Father, to ask you to please alleviate the guilt that is ripping Maggie apart. This guilt is trying to completely destroy her. It is tearing at the very fabric of her soul. This guilt is wrenching her soul to pieces. I am humbly asking you, Father, to please shower Maggie with your unending mercy. Please help her to become strong. Please help her to fight against these memories that are haunting her very soul. Please clear her mind as well as her soul. Maggie did not intentionally sin against you, Father. She was caught up in the evil influence of that man made substance that has ruined so many lives before. Please help her to shine like a beacon in the night for others. Let her testimony be one that others can learn and benefit from, before their lives become so entangled in the sin and heartache that alcohol abuse can bring into their lives. Please help Maggie realize that perhaps some good can come out of all of this. Please, Father, we pray to you in the name of the Father, the Son and the Holy Ghost. Amen!"

Maggie opened her eyes, smiled peacefully over toward her husband, with love in her eyes as she whispered, "Thank you Lord Jesus.......thank you Jesus."

Valerie sat down at her kitchen table and read her father's letter aloud to Lincoln, who sat very quiet and attentive, as each word was uttered.

Valerie began, "Dear Valerie. I realize that it has been a long time since I have tried to make contact with you. I received all of your Christmas cards as well as all of your Birthday greetings over the years. I cannot begin to excuse my behavior. I am truly sorry that I wasn't man enough to let the past be the past and move on. We have lost so many years. We lost good years that we can never attempt to recover. I am so sorry, Valerie. I can never forgive myself for not being there for you when your mother passed away last year. I never stopped loving her, you know. She truly was the finest lady that I have ever known, and it was totally inexcusable for me to leave her like I did. I don't know what possessed me to give up on what we had. Our family was filled with such love and warmth before that incident occurred which tore our family completely apart. I realize now that we could have worked through it, like a family. We could have made it, if I hadn't packed up everything and deserted you and your mother. There is so much from the past that I truly regret. Although I haven't been able to admit it to myself until recently, there is one thing I must tell you. I have missed you so badly over the years. I was in denial concerning my love for you, Valerie. My new wife, Jill, was always after me to contact you. She wanted me to send you a Christmas card or a letter. She was the one who knew what our separation was doing to me. She saw how it was tearing me up inside, even though I was unaware of it.

"Well, just two weeks ago, Jill had a terrible car accident. She lived through it long enough to make a last dying wish. It was more of a prayer, I guess. Just before she slipped away from us, she made me promise that I would try and fix things between us. My eyes became so watery as I made this promise of our reconciliation, that I was unable to focus upon her face as she slipped away from me. Before she died, she heard me agree to contact you and to patch up our wounds. I believe she waited to hear me make this promise before she was at peace long enough to slip away. She never once approved of our estrangement. It always haunted her to no end to think that she was somehow a party to it all, since she married me.

"That brings me to another point. I'd like to tell you that you have a lovely half sister. She is eight years old and she has been the sunshine of my otherwise dreary existence over the course of all these years. Her name is Faith. She loves to watch ballets and she takes piano lessons. She reminds me a lot of you at that age, Valerie. She has your smile and she is every bit as sweet as you are. I am hoping that you will allow us to come up and visit with you in the near future. I love you, Pumpkin! Love, Dad."

Lincoln wiped away at the moisture that had managed to form at the corners of his eyes, as he listened to Valerie read.

"Pumpkin?" Lincoln grinned.

Valerie's face reddened slightly, as she said, "That's what he called me when I was little."

Lincoln laughed, "Well, Pumpkin, where do you go from here?"

Valerie excused herself for a minute as she headed for her bedroom. She explained, "I am going to discuss this with Jesus."

Lincoln sat back and waited for Valerie to get an answer.

Maggie watched her husband disappear from behind the cubicle and then watched him be replaced by Erik Masterson.

"Hello, Erik!" Maggie managed a smile.

Erik reached beneath the glass and shook Maggie's hand, warmly. He said, "I'm so sorry for what you're going through Maggie."

Maggie shook her head, as she said, "No, Erik. I don't need your sympathy. I don't have time for self pity."

Erik let go of Maggie's hand and explained, "I didn't know things were getting this out of control for you, Maggie. If I had known, well then, perhaps we could have handled things differently."

"You're referring to Tyler! Aren't you, Erik?"

Erik nodded, as he said, "Perhaps instead of shipping him off to my sister's family in California, perhaps we could have made other arrangements."

Maggie cried, "Erik! Don't go beating yourself up over this. We did what we thought at the time would be the best thing for him. We weren't married, and you had just gotten engaged to poor Samantha."

"Oh, you heard about how she died?" Erik asked.

"Yes," Maggie admitted, "it's such a shame."

Erik's expression turned quite sad, as he thought about Samantha's demise.

"You loved her didn't you, Erik?"

Erik nodded his head slowly, as he commented, "She was quite a remarkable woman."

Maggie's face began to show signs of concern, as she asked Erik, "How is Helen handling everything?"

Erik replied, "Quite well. She was saved that night, twice. First, she was saved from that assassin's bullet that was intended for her, and then, later on, she prayed at church and was saved from her sins."

"Well, then," Maggie surmised, "this was a case of things turning out for the better."

"Just like your situation, Maggie," Erik suggested. "Some good has got to come out of your situation."

Maggie explained, "It's already started, Erik. Mark and I have never been closer. I have dealt with my demons and through God's grace, I do believe that I am learning how to conquer them."

Erik's face beamed with delight, as he commented, "You know, I think you're right, Maggie. I have never seen you looking so much at peace with yourself. You look simply radiant."

"Well," Maggie laughed softly, "that is the nicest thing that you have ever said to me, Erik Masterson."

Erik laughed, and then a thought suddenly occurred to him, "Why don't I pack up Tyler's things and bring him out here to meet his mother?"

Maggie's expression made a complete turn around, as she shook her head.

"Meet me now? While I'm sitting behind bars? Are you serious, Erik?"

Erik nodded.

"What has he been told about his mother, all of these years?" Maggie asked.

Erik explained, "He knows that my sister is really his Aunt, and he knows that I'm his father."

Maggie repeated her question, "What does my son think has happened to his mother, Erik?"

Erik hung his head low, as he explained, "I struggled with different explanations, over the years, Maggie. I could have lied to the boy any number of ways. In fact, I had thought up at least a million fabrications to spare him from the truth."

"Out with it, Erik!" Maggie demanded.

"I told our son that his mother lived out East and that she led a very different life that did not include us."

Maggie shouted, "Erik! Send for my son, immediately. This is one mess that I think I can clean up."

Scott stood at the door of Shaun's house, ringing the bell. He turned to find several children playing dodge ball in the street. After waiting several more minutes for someone to come to the door, Scott decided to ring the bell once more.

Suddenly, the door flew open and a huge man stood there, towering over Scott like a giant. The smell of hard liquor escaped the interior of the small frame house.

"What do you want, Mister?" The man slurred.

"I'm here to see Shaun and his mother," Scott explained.

"Well, lah-de-dah, Mister. Do you have an appointment?" The man asked, jokingly.

Scott began to feel a bit uneasy, so he went on to explain, "I've been helping Shaun get over his......his troubles."

"Are you a shrink?" The man asked.

Scott laughed, as he said, "No, actually, I'm a journalist."

The man let out an involuntary belch, as he said, "Excuse me, but I don't understand.

What's a journalist want with the kid, here? Are you doing some sort of cover story on juvenile delinquents or something?"

Scott was beginning to lose his patience with the man as he explained, "My profession has nothing to do with why I've been helping Shaun. Could I please come in and see if the boy is all right?"

The man turned his head, glanced back into the house, and then, as he turned back toward Scott, he said, "Look here, Buddy. I'm not gonna let you into this house because I don't know you from Adam. Furthermore, I don't like your style. In fact, I don't think I like you, period. So, make like a bumble bee and fly away. Beat it!"

Scott was stunned, as the man proceeded to slam the door right in his face.

Lucas Lockwood's funeral was restricted to immediate family and close personal friends which did include Chris and Julia.

Chris felt very uneasy and quite agitated during the entire ceremony, as he found himself concentrating upon Lucas' mother, Gloria, and his older sister, Yvonne. He could not read their stonewall expressions. They neither seemed to be grieving nor did they appear to be the least bit distressed over the entire situation. Given the way Lucas left this world, Chris felt that they should at least be showing some sort of loss.

Following the brief graveside ceremony, Lucas' mother walked up to Chris and Julia. She was momentarily joined at her side by Yvonne.

"Chris," Gloria managed a smile as she extended a ring studded hand toward him, "I want to thank you for being a friend to my son over the years."

Chris shook the woman's hand as his eyes began to water, "I'm afraid I didn't have much contact with Lucas throughout the past couple of years, Mrs. Stone."

"Please," the woman smiled once again, "Call me Gloria."

"Gloria," Julia said softly, "we haven't met. My name is Julia. I've been dating Lucas for the past year and a half."

Gloria acted as if there were a foul odor nearby, as she reluctantly shook Julia's hand out of a sense of duty.

Yvonne spoke up from behind her mother, and whispered, "If you and Lucas were dating, Julia, well then, what happened? Weren't you two happy?"

Julia turned toward Yvonne and whispered, "This isn't the time or place to go into this. Perhaps we can all meet somewhere for dinner and discuss matters, then."

Gloria thought for a moment, and then she nodded her head, as she said, "We shall meet tomorrow morning at Lucas' apartment. Yvonne and I require your assistance in cleaning the place up. Is tomorrow morning convenient for the both of you?"

Chris nodded before even giving the matter a second's consideration, but Julia, however, hesitated, as she said, "It's going to be a very painful experience to say the least."

"Aren't you up for the task, young Lady?" Gloria asked condescendingly.

Julia looked over toward Chris and found him nodding his head in encouragement.

"Tomorrow morning it is," Julia agreed.

"Let's make it around nine o'clock," Gloria suggested.

Chris shook Gloria's hand once more and asked, "When will you and Yvonne be flying back to Florida, Gloria?"

Yvonne spoke up before her mother had a chance, and replied, "We're leaving as soon as we can drop off all of Lucas' belongings at the local Goodwill store."

Julia cried softly, "Surely, you're not discarding everything?"

Yvonne challenged Julia by demanding if she had other ideas.

115

"Why," Julia began nervously, "there might be a few things that Chris or I may want to keep as reminders of Lucas."

Gloria spoke up this time, as she placed a hand over Yvonne's opened mouth, "I'm sure that you two shall get exactly what you deserve tomorrow. I foresee no problem, whatsoever."

Later that evening. Lincoln visited his grandmother. He found her wrapped up in a yellow and blue comforter, in bed.

"Gram'," Lincoln called out as he entered the elderly woman's room, "I was wondering if you'd like me to come and pick you up for church Sunday morning?"

MaryFaye's eyes looked bloodshot and watery, as she lay looking up at the ceiling.

As he drew closer, Lincoln realized that his grandmother was in distress.

"Gram'!" He cried out. "What is it? Is it your heart, again?"

MaryFaye struggled to turn her head toward her grandson. Tears began to flow down her face, rapidly, as she realized that she was in too much pain to even perform that menial task.

"Gram'," Lincoln drew closer to her bed. "What should I do? Should I call your doctor?

MaryFaye managed to speak one word, hoarsely, "Water!"

Just as Lincoln turned around to retrieve a glass of water, a young woman entered the room carrying some.

Lincoln watched as this young woman held the glass, steadily, up to MaryFaye's lips.

Lincoln heard the woman's gentle voice, as she whispered, soothingly, into MaryFaye's ears, "Here you go, Mrs. MacWilliams. Drink it slowly, Girl. You don't want to choke."

Lincoln's eyes widened with surprise as he watched this woman with the gentle bedside manner administer to his beloved grandmother.

As the woman placed the empty glass upon the night stand, Lincoln led her to a corner of the room and asked her, "Who are you? Some sort of guardian angel?"

The woman removed Lincoln's grip from her arm and replied, "I'm Marissa, you know, from next door."

Lincoln forgot himself for a minute, as he cried, "Little Marissa? Is it really you? I hardly recognized you."

Marissa warned, Lincoln, "Sh...... I've been trying to get your grandmother to go to sleep."

Lincoln grinned, "Little Marissa? I never would have guessed. You really have grown."

Marissa giggled softly, "That happens to people, you know, Lincoln."

Lincoln continued to grin, as he whispered, "You recognize me!"

Marissa tried to avoid Lincoln's intense staring, by adjusting MaryFaye's pillows. Marissa then turned toward Lincoln, and admitted, "Your grandmother showed me your picture yesterday. I think she was attempting to play matchmaker."

Lincoln turned toward MaryFaye, who was struggling to place a smile upon her face despite the mild physical agony that she was enduring.

CHAPTER FIVE

PARADISE

Erik asked Mark to drop him off at the airport, for he had managed to book a flight to California thanks in large part due to a last minute cancellation. Mark and Erik sat down inside of the airport to talk while Erik awaited his plane's departure.

Mark asked Erik, as he sat down to await the boarding call, "Are you sure you want Tyler to see his mother for the first time, sitting behind bars?"

"It's not my call, Mark," Erik replied. "Maggie was completely adamant about wanting to set things right with her son, before it was too late."

"Too late?" Mark almost shouted. "Why is she talking that way, Erik? Does she know something, that we aren't aware of?"

"No!" Erik reassured the preacher, by placing his hand upon his slightly trembling shoulder.

Mark let out his breath, slowly, and said, "I'm sorry, Erik. I know, I should listen to what I preach. I've never been so scared in my entire life. I can only begin to imagine what this is doing to Maggie and how it might affect your son."

Erik whispered, into Mark's ear, "Let go. Let God."

Mark thanked Erik profusely, and then watched him walk toward the line of people that had just began forming in front of a set of doors which led to the plane.

Just before disappearing from his view, Mark noticed Erik holding up his right thumb and smiling reassuringly toward him.

On that same morning that Erik flew off to California, Shaun awoke from a strange nightmare. He remembered his dream quite vividly. He had awakened from the dream in a heavy coat of perspiration. His scream had brought his mother running into the room.

"What is it, Baby?"

Shaun's forehead was completely soaked as were his night clothes.

Shaun struggled to focus upon his mother's face, despite the beads of perspiration that were trying to invade his eye sockets.

Using a damp wash cloth, Shaun's mother began to wipe away the moisture, as she repeated her question, "What's wrong, Shaun?"

Shaun struggled to speak, as he began to shiver uncontrollably, "I.......I......had, had a nigh....nightmare. I dreamed I was in this...... this crowded room. We were all sitting around in a circle. We were all laughing and talking and stuff. All of a sudden this loud trumpet sounded, and.......and then everyone stopped laughing. They all got quiet. Some people got down on their knees like they were praying or something. The other people just sort of fell flat on their faces, like they were forced to. I stood up and walked around the room, and one by one, the people who knelt down on their own just sort of faded away. The other people started wailing at the top of their lungs, like they were in the worst agony that anyone could ever imagine. Then this roaring fire just suddenly appeared out of nowhere. A voice boomed from above. The voice was talking to me. It said, 'Shaun! Which one will you be?'"

Shaun's mother flipped the rag over and whispered, "We all have silly dreams, Baby."

Shaun sat straight up, and said, "This was no ordinary dream, Mom. It was too intense. I think I heard the voice of God. I think he sent this dream to me as a warning."

Shaun's mother wiped away at his forehead once again, and asked, "A warning? Why would God be warning my Baby?"

Shaun looked at his mother as if he were really seeing her for the first time, as he politely asked her, "Mom, could you please stop calling me Baby?"

Shaun's mother blinked her eyes rapidly for she was taken completely by surprise at the sound of her son's request.

"Sure thing, Baby!" She smiled. "I mean, Shaun."

Suddenly, Shaun and his mother had their attention diverted toward Shaun's bedroom door, where they found Margie's very inebriated boyfriend swaggering in place, while drool ran disgustingly, down his chin.

"What do you want, Raymond?" Margie asked tiredly.

"I want to beat some common sense into that kid of yours, Margie. Someone's got to do it."

Margie stood up, pointed her finger directly into her boyfriend's face, bravely, and said, "If you so much as lay one hand on my son, I promise you that you won't live to regret it, Raymond."

Suddenly, filled with immense anger, Raymond shoved Margie down the hall, causing her to fall to the floor where she knocked her head against the telephone stand.

Raymond began laughing insanely, as he reentered Shaun's room.

Shaun began to try to crawl out of bed for the look in Raymond's eyes was far too familiar to him. He had seen this all before. It was the same look that all of his mother's boyfriends gave him, right before they beat the living daylights out of him.

As Shaun stepped down onto the floor, Raymond closed the door with one mighty slam.

Shaun started to think about his friend, Scott, the only man in his life who had actually been kind to him without any ulterior motives in mind. Shaun's final thought, before Raymond threw a near fatal blow to his head was, of the time he awoke to find Scott praying for him.

Just before he lost all consciousness, Shaun heard his mother's blood curdling scream.

Chris and Julia stood outside of Lucas' apartment waiting for Yvonne and Gloria to arrive.

Chris glanced at his watch for the twelfth time in the past fifteen minutes.

"Maybe they got caught in traffic, Chris," Julia suggested.

Chris began to run his fingers, nervously, through his hair as he paced up and down the sidewalk.

"Why are you so nervous, Chris?" Julia asked.

Chris replied, "I don't know. I guess Lucas' mother and his sister make me feel a little uneasy, I guess."

Julia nodded her head as she agreed, "I know what you mean, Chris. They both acted a little indifferent about the whole thing, that's for sure."

Chris glanced up the street, saw that it was deserted and then he turned toward Julia and said, "I've always wondered why they left Lucas here after Gloria and his father split up. She left Lucas alone with a man who was entirely impossible to please."

Julia began to recall past conversations that she had with Lucas whenever the subject of his father came up.

She recalled one in particular. She shared with Chris, "I remember a story that Lucas once told me about when he was in the fourth grade and he had made his father a small sailboat out of clay in art class. Lucas' father took one look at the thing, and immediately, he began to criticize it, saying, 'Boy, you got the sail way too big for the proportion of the boat. If someone were to use this model for a real boat, why the thing would topple over at the slightest breeze.'

"Lucas' heart was crushed to pieces, as he watched his father toss his project into the garbage, saying, 'Back to the drawing board, Son.'"

Chris stopped pacing as he told Julia, "I never heard that one."

Julia asked Chris, "What? Do you have another story?"

Chris replied, "Yes, I remember once, when Lucas was drowning his sorrows with a six pack of beer, he told me this story about him and his father going on a camping trip with a bunch of Lucas' friends and their fathers. Lucas told me how proud and excited he was that he was finally going to spend some quality time with his father. He told me how his father had completely changed around his schedule in order to join him on this trip."

"What happened?" Julia asked, although she felt afraid to hear the rest.

"Well," Chris continued, "it seems after a full day of fishing and hiking, everyone decided to sit around the campfire. It was late at night and they decided to tell ghost stories. Everyone was really getting into the mood. They were all really bonding with one another. Well, one kid decided to ask Lucas' father to tell a story. Lucas became real excited about the whole idea that it was his father's turn to entertain everyone. The anticipation was growing rapidly inside of Lucas' mind, as his father prepared his story. After making sure that each boy sitting around the campfire had a marshmallow firmly hanging on their sticks, his father began to tell his story. Lucas glanced around the circle of his friends in order to drink in their excitement. He watched their eyes open wide with all sorts of anticipation, and then, Lucas' heart sank once again, as he heard his father say, 'Boys, this here is not a ghost story, however, it is a true story. My son Lucas, here is an avid fisherman. One time when he was about ten years old, Lucas accompanied myself and my law partner on a trip to Mosquito Lake. Mind you, this was Lucas' first time on a boat. We took my partner's boat way out to the middle of the lake.

"By the time we made it out to the middle, Lucas' face was as white as a ghost. He looked like he was going to lose his lunch, at any moment. Well, unfortunately, for us that day the fish were just not biting. Lucas, here, came up with a solution for us. My son bent over the side of the boat and blew his chunks. All kinds of fish surfaced as they feasted upon Lucas' regurgitated morsels. Needless to say, the fish began to bite.'

"All the other kids began to howl in laughter, at Lucas' expense. I guess Lucas had turned all sorts of red, as he ran out into the woods in order to escape his unexpected humiliation."

"That's terrible, Chris. How could a father do that to his own son?"

Chris shrugged and then he whispered, "I bet Lucas had a million more stories just like that one."

Suddenly, Chris glanced back down the street and observed a bright yellow car pulling up to a nearby curb.

"They're here, Julia," Chris announced, as he watched Lucas' mother and sister emerge from the automobile.

Margie felt immense pain in the back of her head, as she struggled to get to her feet. After tremendous effort, she managed to reach the telephone, which had been knocked clear across the floor. With shaking fingers, she dialed 911. After a voice came on the other end, Margie began to babble, incoherently.

A loud noise caused her to accidentally hang up the receiver. She crouched down in a corner and began to shake, uncontrollably, as she feared the worst.

As Julia unlocked the door to Lucas' apartment, Gloria asked her, "Were you sleeping with my son, Julia?"

Julia shot Chris a concerned glance, as she attempted to give Gloria a reply.

Yvonne spoke up, "Never mind, Julia. Your expression speaks loud enough."

Julia took in a deep breath as she opened the door. Stepping aside, Julia allowed Gloria and Yvonne to enter in. Chris followed the ladies trying to avoid Julia's glare.

"Well, where do we start?" Gloria turned toward Chris and Julia after quickly surveying the room.

Julia suggested, "We could start with Lucas' bedroom."

Gloria gave Yvonne a questioning look, as they followed Julia into the bedroom.

After they all entered the room, Julia explained, "This is where Lucas stored everything."

Gloria's eyebrows lifted slightly, as she watched Julia open a closet door.

Upon realizing that Julia was about to pick up some boxes, Chris made his way to the closet, and intervened, as he said, "Allow me, Julia."

Gloria and Yvonne stood against a far wall with their arms folded in front of them, watching Chris and Julia drag out box after box.

Julia began to pull back the flaps in order to peer inside of them.

Yvonne watched with total disgust as Chris and Julia began poking around inside of the boxes.

Gloria glanced over toward her daughter and rolled her eyes.

"You both are behaving like total scavengers. Why don't we simply seal up all of these boxes and deliver them to the Goodwill store?"

Julia began to lose her patience, as she suddenly stood up, and walked over toward Yvonne.

Standing directly in front of the woman, Julia spoke in a serious tone, "You never bothered to get to know your brother while he was alive. It seems to me that it would only be proper for you to try to get to know him, now. Going through his things, is the only way you have left to know him. He really was a great guy. It's only too bad you never took the time to notice."

Yvonne turned toward her mother and asked, "Can she speak to me like that, Mother?"

Gloria smiled a strange smile, as she replied, "Sure she can, Yvonne. She was your dead brother's lover. She can speak to you any way she pleases."

Julia threw her arms up in the air, as she returned to the box that she had begun to examine.

Rico walked beside Alice as she pushed their son in a stroller that Valerie had purchased for them. Up ahead, Rico noticed a group of his friends gathered around a street vendor.

"What's up, Rico?" A man wearing a red bandanna over his otherwise bald head, called out.

"Gregorio! When did you blow back into town?" Rico asked, as he and the man exchanged their special handshake.

"Last night, Man!" Gregorio answered. As he looked down at the baby, he whistled and said, "Things sure have changed around here, Man."

Rico smiled proudly, "I'll say! Take a good look here at my son, Gregorio. Ain't he something?"

Gregorio knelt down and took a closer look, and then he laughed as he said, "He's your kid all right, Rico. Just take a look at that nose."

Alice defiantly spoke up, "I think it's a very honorable nose."

Gregorio stood back up, and apologized, "I'm sorry, Alice. I wasn't putting your baby down. I think, in time, the little guy should grow into it. In fact, Rico is still growing into his."

Everyone laughed, at Rico's expense, which caused him to turn red.

One of the gang member's shouted, "Hey, Rico! Is fatherhood gonna keep you home every night, now? Did we lose our fearless leader to diapers and baby formula?"

Rico glanced over at Alice out of the corner of his eye, and then he replied, "I'm afraid so, guys. This kid, here, means the world to me. I think he's kind of changed me or something."

Another gang member shouted, "I don't believe it. Who would have thought it would be Alice who would get her fingernails into Rico's skin? I would have laid odds on Heather Fairchild."

Gregorio turned toward the gang and asked, "Is that rich chick still available? Maybe I should pay the fair maiden a little visit and turn on my charm."

Alice laughed, "What charm, Gregorio? You couldn't charm a snake."

Gregorio grinned, as he asked, "How would you know, Pretty Lady?"

Alice responded, "I don't know, Gregorio. And believe me, I wouldn't want to know."

Gregorio began to get restless. He turned toward the gang, and suggested, "Why don't we all go over to Mulligan's and shoot some pool?"

After they all agreed, Gregorio turned toward Rico and Alice, and asked, "Would you three care to join us?"

Alice replied, "Oh, right, Gregorio. I'm sure a bar is the best place for a baby."

Gregorio directed his question to Rico, "How about it, Rico? It'll be just like old times."

At first, Rico resisted his first impulse to accept the invitation, but when Alice gave her reluctant approval, he accepted.

"I won't be home late, Honey."

A mocking voice from the crowd, using a high pitched tone, shouted, "Bring home some milk and bread, Dear."

Again, everyone laughed, including Alice and Rico.

Valerie stood on MaryFaye's front porch ringing the doorbell, when the door finally opened, revealing to her a small thin woman.

"Oh, excuse me, but I'm here to see Lincoln and MaryFaye."

The woman replied harshly, "You didn't need to keep on pushing that bell. I finally got Mrs. MacWilliams to fall asleep."

Valerie blushed slightly, as she apologized, "I'm sorry. I didn't know."

The woman was joined by Lincoln who pushed past her to extend his hand toward Valerie. As he ushered her inside, he whispered, "Valerie, this is Marissa. Marissa, this here's Valerie. She's a nurse, and a very good friend of mine."

Marissa suspiciously eyed Valerie, as she watched the way Lincoln acted around her. Marissa immediately decided, that she did not care for Valerie.

"My grandmother is ill, again, Valerie," Lincoln explained softly, "I'm afraid it might be her heart."

"Shouldn't we send for an ambulance?" Valerie asked.

Marissa spoke up, "I've been caring for Mrs. MacWilliams, Valerie."

Valerie smiled politely toward Marissa and then she turned back toward Lincoln and continued, "Your grandmother may require professional medical assistance."

Lincoln asked Valerie, "Could you stick around until she wakes up, Valerie?"

Valerie glanced at her wrist watch, and said, "Yes, Lincoln, I can stay, but I have to be at the airport this evening."

Lincoln's eyes widened with excitement, "Are you picking up your father at the airport?"

Valerie nodded, excitedly, as she added, "And my little sister."

Marissa crossed her arms, sternly, as she watched Lincoln and Valerie embrace one another.

Margie attempted once more to call for help. Her eyes would not focus for she had begun to cry hysterically.

"Margie?" A male voice from somewhere inside of the house called out.

Margie replaced the receiver, as she attempted to retreat back to the corner.

Once again, a man's voice called out, "Margie? Is everything all right?"

Margie watched in horror as a man entered the hallway where she sat in a corner, trembling.

"Margie, it's me, Scott."

Margie struggled to her feet as she made her way down the hall.

Scott took Margie's trembling body into his arms and asked, "What happened, Margie? Is Shaun all right."

Margie struggled to speak, "No, he.....he's in there...I'm afraid he might be dead."

Scott rushed off into the direction of Shaun's room, pushed the door open, and discovered Shaun's body draped, helplessly, over his bed rail. Blood was pouring from his mouth, forming a pool on his blue rug.

Margie entered the room, took in the gruesome sight of her son and then, she fainted.

MaryFaye stirred from her sleep. As she slowly opened her eyes, she spotted Lincoln, Marissa and Valerie smiling down at her.

"Well, hello, Sunshine!" Lincoln grinned.

MaryFaye smiled, as she said, "Your grandfather liked to call me Sunshine. I miss him so much. I have this feeling that I will be joining him soon."

Marissa said soothingly, "Nonsense, Mrs. MacWIliams. You've still got a lot of living to do."

MaryFaye shook her head slowly, and whispered, "No I don't little girlfriend. I'm afraid my time down here on earth is drawing to a close. Don't worry, Child. I have no regrets. I've lived a good, long life. The good Lord has blessed me over the years."

Lincoln smiled and whispered, "The Lord has blessed us with you, Gram'."

MaryFaye smiled contentedly, as Lincoln placed a warm kiss upon her cheek.

Chris pulled out a small trophy and showed it to Yvonne and laughed, as he said, "See this? Lucas won this one year when we joined a bowling league. Lucas couldn't bowl a good game if his life depended upon it."

Yvonne knelt down beside Chris and asked, "Well, then, how did he win this trophy?"

"Look closer," Julia laughed, softly.

Yvonne peered at the inscription and then she smiled, as she read, "Worst score!"

Gloria pretended not to care as the others laughed at the trophy which was of a bowler who had dropped the ball onto his foot.

Yvonne peered into the box and pulled out an old photograph that was in a gold frame. A tear came to her eye when she gazed at the photo which had been taken the year before her parents had split up. In the picture, she was only eight years old and Lucas was only four. Her parents appeared to be quite happy in the picture.

Gloria asked to see the picture.

Yvonne handed it over to her mother and then wiped away at the tear.

Gloria attempted to keep her composure as she gazed upon the photo.

After a minute passed by, Gloria ordered, "Destroy it!"

Yvonne retrieved the picture, and said, "You'll do no such thing, Mother. I'm going to keep it."

"Well," Gloria fumed, "I don't ever want to see it again!"

Chris pulled out a small stuffed animal. It was quite worn. He held it up and asked the ladies, "Do either of you recognize this?"

Yvonne shook her head no, while still gazing upon the small photograph.

Gloria reached out for the small stuffed bear, and cried, "Binky! After all of these years, he still held onto Binky!"

Julia watched as Gloria wept into the brown bear. It's stuffing was falling out, around one ear.

Yvonne looked up and watched her mother lose complete control of her emotions.

"That bear must have been special," Julia whispered.

Gloria cried, "My brother bought this for Lucas on the day that he was born."

Yvonne asked, "Uncle Reggie?"

Gloria nodded.

Julia asked, "Who was Uncle Reggie?"

Yvonne explained, "He was my mother's youngest brother. He came to visit at the hospital when Lucas was born. After his visit, on the way home from the hospital, Uncle Reggie was involved in a car accident. He was killed instantly."

For the first time, Julia and Chris began to feel some remorse for Gloria. They began to realize that the woman obviously did have feelings bottled up inside of her, that were now just beginning to come to the surface.

Valerie stood in the airport terminal reading the screen which hung high in the air. She discovered that her father's flight from Florida would be arriving in about ten minutes at Gate 4A.

As she began to walk down the corridor, she began to think about the telephone conversation that she had with him last night. He had said, "It's great to hear your voice, Valerie. We have so much to catch up on. I'm so sorry for all of the wasted years. I wish you could have met Jill. You really would have liked her."

Valerie grinned, as she neared the gate. She sat down and began to watch a pair of boys as they chased one another around the room. An airline pilot stopped to talk to a ticket agent. A young couple whispered to one another. The man wore a cowboy hat, and the woman wore her hair in braids. An elderly woman walked along with the aid of a cane. A tall man, in faded blue jeans stopped at a drinking fountain to quench his thirst. A middle aged man, quite distinguished looking, in his gray suit, stood in front of Valerie grinning. A young, frail girl with long flowing, blonde hair stood beside him, holding his hand, tightly. She appeared to be a bit frightened and withdrawn.

"Valerie," the man said with a smile.

Valerie jumped up from her seat, and asked, "Dad? Is it really you? You're so gray now."

The man laughed, "You are so beautiful, Valerie. Come here, give your old man a hug."

Valerie hugged her father tightly, and then, after releasing her grip, she looked back down at the little girl.

"This must be Faith!" Valerie smiled warmly.

The little girl held out her thin arm toward Valerie and said, "I'm pleased to meet you."

Valerie gently shook the girl's hand. Laughing she said, "Well, I'm very pleased to meet you, too."

A voice came over the public address system. It announced, 'Courtesy call for Frank Rhodes.'

"Who knows you're here, Dad?" Valerie asked, as the three of them headed for a telephone.

"I contacted my old business partner. If things work out, Faith and I may move here, permanently."

Valerie whispered, under her breath, "Thank you, Jesus!"

Scott suggested to Margie, that she stop pacing the floor of the emergency waiting room, and sit down.

Margie cried softly, "How can I just sit, Scott? My baby boy may be dying, and it's all my fault for bringing home trashy men all the time."

Scott rubbed Margie's neck in order to relieve some of the pressure that she was feeling.

"How long has he been in there?" Margie asked nervously.

Scott looked at his watch and replied, "Two hours."

"They ought to be able to tell us something, by now," Margie cried.

"You stay put, Margie," Scott ordered. "I'll go speak to the nurse."

Just as Scott rose from his seat, a man in a white jacket, approached them.

The man extended his hand, and said, "I'm Dr. Kanaly. Are you the boy's father?"

Scott shook his head, and said, "No! But this, here, is Shaun's mother."

The doctor reintroduced himself to Margie and then he said, "Your son is very, very lucky to be alive, Ma'am. His condition, however, is very grave."

"Grave?" Margie swallowed hard, fighting back tears which were waiting for the right time to come gushing down her cheeks.

"Yes," the doctor continued, "I'm afraid the blow to his head was very severe. He lost a lot of blood. We are monitoring him for any internal bleeding. I suggest you both get some rest. It's going to be awhile before we can tell you anything further."

Margie fell into Scott's arms as if she were a rag doll. Scott helped her over to a chair, and for the first time he realized how frail she looked. Her face was as white as a ghost. Underneath her eyes, he noticed dark circles that she had tried to cover up with makeup.

Scott suggested, "Margie, you don't look so good. Maybe we ought to get a doctor to examine you."

Margie threw her left arm up, helplessly, as she whispered, "Whatever! I am pretty tired."

Scott ushered a nurse over to the side and whispered to her, while pointing at Margie's slumped over body.

The nurse went into action, quickly, by retrieving a wheel chair from a corner.

Scott assisted the nurse as they helped Margie into it.

Margie looked around after she was seated in the wheel chair. She smiled as she said, "And, we're off!"

Alice placed her baby in his crib and then she stepped quietly out of his room. Walking toward the living room of her apartment, Alice glanced over at the small digital clock, which sat upon the small black and white television.

"Twelve thirty!" Alice whispered obviously disappointed.

As she sat down, she picked up the Bible that Valerie had given her. It was a huge Life Application Bible. She turned to the back of the Bible and found the Index. She flipped through the pages and then she stopped at the word, 'worry'.

The index indicated a passage of scripture that she felt might be of encouragement to her as she waited patiently for Rico's safe return home.

Alice decided to read the first few verses of Psalm 37. She read, "Never envy the wicked! Soon they fade away like grass and disappear. Trust in the Lord instead. Be kind and good to others; then you will live safely here in the land and prosper, feeding in safety. Be delighted with the Lord. Then he will give you all your heart's desires. Commit everything you do to the Lord. Trust him to help you do it and he will. Your innocence will be clear to everyone. He will vindicate you with the blazing light of justice shining down as from the noonday sun. Rest in the Lord; wait patiently for him to act. Don't be envious of evil men who prosper. Stop your anger! Turn off your wrath. Don't fret and worry, it only leads to harm. For the wicked shall be destroyed, but those who trust the Lord shall be given every blessing, and shall have wonderful peace."

Alice got down on her knees, after she closed her Bible. She folded her hands in true submission to her Lord and Savior.

She began to pray, "Dear Lord. I confess to you that I am truly worried about Rico. I know that you want us to place our trust in you. That is what I am doing now, Lord. I am placing all of my cares and worries at your precious feet, Lord. I pray that you will deliver Rico safely home to me. I pray that you will help him to leave his past behind and start the rest of his life serving you, Lord. In Jesus' precious name we pray. Amen."

Just as Alice was rising to her feet, the door flew open, and Rico stumbled in. His breath reeked with alcohol. He was crying profusely. Alice reached out to him, but he pushed her away.

He cried, "Don't touch me, Alice, I'm dirt! I'm dirt, Alice! You're white as snow, and I'm dirt! I don't deserve you and our baby. I'm dirt!"

Alice watched, helplessly, as Rico fell on the floor in a heap.

After closing the door, Alice knelt down beside Rico, who was still crying uncontrollably.

"What is it, Rico?" She asked.

"Nothing!" Rico said as he wiped away at his nose with his hand.

"Tell me what happened, Rico!" Alice demanded.

Rico looked up at Alice with extremely bloodshot eyes, and said, "Gregorio went crazy. He drank a few shots. He guzzled a few beers. We played some pool. We even sang a little karaoke, tonight. And then, Gregorio lost it. He completely lost it. He pulled out this gun. No one knew he had a gun. We were all sitting around this table having a good time and Gregorio suddenly pulls out this gun out of nowhere. He starts shooting up the place. He shot the bartender. He shot the barmaid. He shot the young couple playing pool. He even shot the karaoke singer and the guy running the show. He shot the entire gang. He killed everybody, Alice! And then, he pointed the gun down my throat. He even cocked back on the trigger. I tell you Alice, I was never so scared in my life. He looked me straight in the eyes and he said, "Rico, I'm going to let you live. You got a boy to raise, so I'm going to let you live. After he said that, he just turned the gun on himself and pulled the trigger. He blew his head off right there in front of me."

Alice's eyes teared up so badly, she couldn't control herself.

"How could he do that Rico? How could he shoot those people, all those innocent people? How could he shoot his friends? He must have been possessed, or something."

Rico attempted to regain his composure, but the memory of the shooting returned to him, vividly. Rico lost control of his emotions once again, as he cried relentlessly.

Valerie tucked Faith into bed, and smiled down at her, and said, "It's going to be fun to have a little sister around. We can go shopping together. We can eat ice cream, maybe go to the movies. It's going to be great."

Faith asked Valerie, "Could you please stay here while I say my prayers?"

"Of course, Faith," Valerie said, as she sat down upon the little girl's bed. Faith folded her hands together, closed her eyes, and began to pray, "Heavenly Father, first of all, I want to thank you for bringing me and Papa here. I think I am really going to like it. I want to thank you for my sister. She is real pretty and nice. Please tell my Mama that I miss her terribly. Tell her not to worry about me. Tell her that it won't be long now. Give her a hug for me. In Jesus' name we pray. Amen."

Valerie shut off the light and turned to leave, when she stopped to ask Faith, "What did you mean by it won't be long now?"

From somewhere in the darkness, Faith replied calmly, "It won't be long before I see my Mama, again."

Valerie left the door to Faith's room open as she left. Walking toward the living room, Valerie found her father on the couch, reading a newspaper.

Valerie sat beside her father, and whispered, "Is Faith sick, Dad?"

Frank placed the paper down and looked Valerie straight in the eyes, and replied, "The doctors give her merely weeks to live. Her illness has advanced rapidly, ever since her mother passed on. It seems she's lost the will to live. I'm losing my baby."

Valerie watched tears form in her father's eyes for the first time in her life. In the past, Frank Rhodes never ever lost his composure.

Valerie asked, "Isn't there anything they can do for her, Dad?"

Frank wiped away at his uncharacteristic tears as he whispered, "No! They've tried everything. There's nothing else left for them to do. They just said to keep her happy and comfortable."

Valerie hugged her father tightly and cried, "I'll be here for you, Dad, when the time comes."

Frank released his daughter and gazed into her eyes and asked her, "Do you think God is punishing me for what I did to you, Val?"

Valerie shook her head, as she replied, "No! I don't think so, Dad. They say good comes out of everything for those who love God."

Lincoln and Marissa grew concerned for MaryFaye when her breathing began to get heavy, so they decided to take her to the hospital that evening.

In the emergency room, Lincoln ran into Scott. He was nervously pacing the floor.

"Why are you here, Lincoln?" Scott asked.

Lincoln ran his hand, nervously, over his forehead, and replied, "My grandmother is very ill, Scott."

"Oh, I'm sorry to hear that, Man."

Marissa walked up behind Lincoln and placed a reassuring hand upon his shoulder, and said, "I guess your friend, Valerie, was right after all, Lincoln. I'm so sorry that we didn't get your grandmother here, earlier."

Scott held his hand out to Marissa and said, "Hi. My name's Scott. I'm a friend of Lincoln's."

Marissa shook Scott's hand and said, "Well, any friend of Lincoln's has got to be pretty special, too. I'm glad to meet you. I'm Marissa."

"I'm pleased to meet you, Marissa. I wish we had met under better circumstances."

"Yes!" Marissa agreed. "Why are you here, Scott?"

"A young friend of mine is here."

"Oh," Marissa sympathized, "I hope it isn't too serious."

"I'm afraid it's touch and go. He might not make it through the night."

Lincoln intervened, out of concern, "It's not Shaun, again, is it, Scott?"

"I'm afraid so, Lincoln," Scott admitted.

"That poor kid. He's been through so much in his short life."

Scott glanced around and spotted the nurse that had gone off with Margie, earlier.

"Excuse me," Scott begged, as he headed straight for the nurse who was looking at a chart.

The nurse looked up and asked, "Can I help you?"

"How is Margie Collins?" Scott asked.

"She's resting comfortably. They ran some tests on her. We have our own lab. We should have the results, soon."

Scott turned back toward Lincoln and Marissa and explained to them, "Shaun's mother is being seen by a doctor, also."

"What's wrong with her, Scott?" Lincoln asked.

Scott shrugged and replied, "I'm not sure. But given her track record with men, there's no telling what might be wrong with her. She looks awful."

Chris and Julia spent the entire day going through Lucas' things. The whole ordeal took an emotional toll out on everyone.

Gloria discovered that Lucas and she had more in common than she had been aware of, before. She discovered that Lucas enjoyed growing plants and flowers.

She nearly fell over in surprise when she found Lucas' flower garden out on the patio. The garden contained her favorite flowers.

Yvonne never let go of the photograph and she also took a special interest in a loose leaf journal that Lucas had been keeping. Julia wasn't even aware of it's existence. After agreeing upon what was to be given away to charity and what would be divided up amongst themselves, the four departed company.

It was late that night, when Chris told Julia, "I need to be alone, for awhile."

Julia understood and went home to her apartment.

Chris walked along the streets of downtown looking into the plate glass windows of all of the shops along the way.

Chris came upon a tavern where he heard laughter and music playing.

He felt so alone and depressed that he thought to himself, "I need to laugh again. I need to hear music. Most of all, I need to escape all those memories that were conjured up, today. I can always drink something that's non-alcoholic."

Chris entered the bar and immediately, he began to feel out of place. As he sat down on a bar stool, Chris found himself ordering a Coke. As he sat there sipping his drink, he discovered that those memories that he was attempting to escape simply were not going away. He tried to concentrate on the music that was blaring from the jukebox. It was playing music that he used to listen to, when he was younger and much more wild. Strangely enough, he didn't seem to enjoy this music like he used to.

Chris became lost in thought, so deeply, that he didn't realize that a young woman had sat down beside him. As the smell of her cheap perfume permeated his nostrils, Chris turned to face the young woman.

"Hi there, Stranger!"

Chris asked, blankly, "Are you talking to me?"

The young woman giggled, "You're cute! Do you party?"

Chris looked straight ahead, trying not to reveal how nervous and out of place he was feeling.

"When a girl asks you a question you're supposed to answer her!"

Chris noticed that the girl's tone of voice was getting louder. He did not wish to attract undue attention toward himself, so he decided to attempt to appease the girl for it seemed she was starving for attention or something else, entirely.

"No! I don't party," Chris replied.

The girl leaned back in her bar stool, and stretched her legs. With a slight yawn, she said, "That's too bad. What do you do? Do you fool around?"

Chris felt himself turning twenty shades of red as he tried to avoid the girl's feminine wiles.

"Well?" The girl asked, impatiently. "I haven't got all night you know. I have to be at work in the morning."

Chris turned toward the girl and said, "Look here. I came into this place to relax, not to be harassed. So if you'll just take your pretty little face back to that jukebox and leave me alone, we'll both be better off."

The girl took this to be a challenge instead of being turned off by it, as she said, "Excuse me!"

Chris began to feel annoyed, for the girl refused to leave his side.

The girl forced Chris to look her straight in the eyes, and tell her that he wanted her to leave.

As Chris stared into her baby blue eyes, he became entranced by them. He sensed a feeling of loneliness in them. He saw how she had endured so much rejection, just by looking in them.

He suddenly began to feel sorry for her.

"There's something different about you," the young woman observed. "There's something holy about you. What are you doing in a dive like this?"

Chris responded, before he realized what he was saying, "I came in here to drown my sorrows."

The girl, then stood up, pulled out a few dollar bills, and called for the bartender, "Hey, Leo. Come here when you get the chance. I want to buy my new friend here something."

Chris began to sip through the straw faster, while, nervously watching the girl order him a shot of Tequila.

Chris shook his head, as he protested, "No. You don't need to do that."

The girl placed the shot in Chris' hand and then she picked hers up, and said, "Come on! Bottoms up! You said you came in here to drown your sorrows. They won't even go under once, with Coke."

Reluctantly, Chris followed his old ways, by swallowing the shot of Tequila.

The liquor went down hard and painfully. Chris felt tremendous guilt. But after being coaxed into another shot, all of Chris' feelings of regret seemed to dissipate, at least temporarily.

In the middle of the night Faith began to complain about stomach cramps. Valerie awoke first to the sound of Faith's groaning.

As she entered the room, Valerie went directly over to Faith's bed to feel her forehead.

"You're burning up, Faith!" Valerie cried out.

Faith cried, slightly, "The doctor said this might be a side effect from the medication they put me on."

Valerie left the room and momentarily returned with a thermometer.

By this time, Frank awoke, and was sitting on Faith's bed, stroking her hair which was damp with perspiration.

"Dad, I think she has a fever," Valerie suggested, as she placed the thermometer underneath Faith's tongue.

"Maybe the plane ride was too rough for her."

Valerie shook her head, and said, "I don't think so, Dad."

Faith tried to give her father a reassuring smile, but she found the pain in her stomach was too great for her to force a smile.

Dr. Kanaly raced up to Scott and informed him, "Shaun has slipped into a coma."

"A coma?" Scott asked, being caught completely off guard.

"Yes, I'm afraid so. We're monitoring him very closely."

Scott ran his fingers through his hair as he walked over to Lincoln who was attempting to purchase a snack from a vending machine.

"I'm so nervous, Scott. I can't even count out sixty cents in change."

Scott looked Lincoln straight in the eyes and said, "Shaun's in a coma, Lincoln."

Lincoln dropped all of his change to the floor and then he gave Scott a quick hug.

Marissa stepped over to the machine and began to pick up Lincoln's change for him.

"Thanks, Marissa!" Lincoln said.

Marissa handed over the change to Lincoln and asked, "Why won't they let us go to see her, Lincoln? What could they be doing to her?"

Lincoln replied, "I'm sure she's in good hands, Marissa."

Maggie Jensen stared at the ceiling from her narrow cot. She began to imagine the faces of loved ones carved in the ceiling.

The first such face to appear to her, was that of her mother, who had passed away when Maggie was eighteen. The image of her mother was so clear, that Maggie noticed her mother was crying.

Maggie whispered, "I'm so sorry, Mama. I've been real bad. Do you remember the time that I borrowed your pearl necklace without asking you? I was determined to wear them to the prom. I hid them in my purse until I got into Erik's car. You never suspected a thing, did you, Mama?"

Maggie watched as the image of her mother began to fade away.

"Don't go, Mama. Don't go, yet," Maggie cried.

The image returned, briefly.

Maggie continued, "Well, Mama, I remember how you felt when I confessed to borrowing them. You were so crushed. You told me about how disappointed in me you were. You told me that you had lost all trust in me. I explained how I lost them. The string broke suddenly sending your precious pearls down to the street below. I explained, how they managed to find their way down a sewer drain. You just stood there, staring at me. I was so hurt by your stare. You never felt the same toward me, since that day. I'm sorry, Mama."

Maggie watched the image of her mother fade away. The next image to appear to Maggie was that of her grandmother, who had been dead for ten years. This image appeared to be very calm and serene.

"Grandma, is that really you?" Maggie whispered, as she fought to choke back additional tears.

Chris stumbled off of his bar stool, and started for the door.

"You're not driving, are you, St. Christopher?"

Chris turned around, abruptly, and faced the young girl who had been steadily supplying him with shots of Tequila. Chris waved his index finger in her face, and explained, "My full name is Christian, not St. Christopher."

The young woman giggled, "Well, you're a real mess, Christian. I sure hope you don't run into any of your church friends."

Chris placed his hand over his mouth and, in mock embarrassment, he cried out, "Hide me!"

The young woman helped Chris outside where the cool, crisp night air hit them both like a cold wash rag on their faces.

Chris stuttered, "Love....love...lovely weather we're having."

The young woman giggled, "Where are we headed, Romeo?"

Chris glanced off in several directions and thought for a minute, before deciding upon a choice.

"That way!" Chris demanded, as he started to head south, down the street.

As Chris took off, the girl shouted, "Hey, Christian! I want to go wherever you're headed!"

Chris turned around, and called out, "We're going to see paradise, ah.......what's your name, anyway?"

The girl giggled, "I thought you'd never ask. My name's Diana."

Maggie watched as the image of her grandmother floated against the white background of the prison ceiling.

"Grandma, it's good to see you. I loved you because you always let me be myself. You never judged me, Grandma. I always loved you for that."

Maggie's eyes began to clear up a bit, as she gazed upon the image of her grandmother's kind face.

Valerie and her father hurried Faith, who had been placed in a wheelchair immediately upon their arrival, through the emergency door, at Mercy Hospital.

A nurse rushed up to Frank and asked, "What's happened, Sir?"

Frank explained, nervously, "My daughter has contracted the Aids virus through a blood transfusion."

Valerie shot her father a concerned glance, as she heard the name of Faith's illness for the first time.

After Frank and Valerie discussed the symptoms that Faith was exhibiting, with the nurse, the young girl was whisked away, down a long corridor.

Frank turned away from Valerie's eyes, which were filling up with tears.

"Daddy," Valerie cried. "It really didn't hit me, until now. We're really going to lose that precious little angel."

"Oh," Frank cried. "I wish that you two could have had more time to get to know each other."

Valerie hugged her father's neck and said, soothingly, "Soon, she'll be in Heaven with Jesus."

Frank wrestled free from his eldest daughter's warm embrace and then he walked over to a corner where he stood, sobbing quietly.

Valerie glanced around the waiting room and spotted Scott and Lincoln standing near the nurse's station.

"Hey, you guys. What's going on?" Valerie asked, while attempting to wipe away the tears that were falling down her cheeks.

Lincoln gave Valerie a hug, as he explained, "I think that my grandmother is pretty sick, Val."

Valerie gave Scott a questioning look, as she released Lincoln's embrace.

Scott explained, "I'm here, because Shaun had a run in with another one of his mother's boyfriends. He's in pretty bad shape."

Valerie shrugged, helplessly, as she whispered under her breath, "When it rains, it pours."

Marissa walked up to the trio of friends and asked Valerie, "Why are you here, Valerie? Are you on duty?"

Valerie replied, "No, Marissa. My little sister is quite ill, I'm afraid."

Scott asked, "Is that your father over there Valerie? We'd all love to meet him."

Valerie turned toward the corner where her father was standing, and then she became alarmed at the sight of the older man as he collapsed to the floor.

MaryFaye laid comfortably in her hospital bed glancing out at the night air. She smiled warmly remembering the autumns of her youth. She and her father used to pick blueberries, together. Afterward, her mother would bake her fabulous pies.

MaryFaye was completely lost in thought, when a couple of nurses entered the room to check up on her.

"How are you feeling, Mrs. MacWilliams?"

MaryFaye jumped a bit, and then she replied, "You scared me. I didn't even hear you two come into the room."

"Oh, we're sorry, Mrs. MacWilliams," the nurse apologized. "I told the administrators that they ought to issue each of us a set of cowbells to hang around our necks."

MaryFaye managed a polite giggle, as she asked, "How long before I get to have visitors, Nurse?"

The nurse who had been carrying a tray of syringes and several tubes for drawing blood, replied, cheerily, "As soon as the doctor gives his permission. He'll be in here, shortly."

"Is there anything we can get you, now, Mrs. MacWlliams?"

MaryFaye thought for a minute and then answered, "Yes, could you send for Pastor Mark Jensen, please? I'd like to see him, before I go."

The two nurses shot each other concerned glances, at the sound of MaryFaye's request.

Diana allowed Chris to lean against her as he directed their path.

"Aren't you going to tell me where we're headed, Christian?"

Chris stumbled a bit, giggled, and then he answered, "I told you. We're going to Paradise."

Diana helped Chris regain his footing and then she spotted something up ahead. It began to slightly scare her.

Chris noticed Diana's strange look and it sent him off on a laughing spree, which grew to be uncontrollable and a bit hysterical.

"There," he nodded excitedly, "yes, yes there it is. Sweet Paradise!"

Diana watched as Chris broke free of her and clumsily run straight for a bridge which overlooked a river.

Calling back over his shoulder, Chris shouted, "This was Lucas' favorite place to go and think."

Raindrops began to fall slowly as Diana ran after Chris. She called out, "Who in the world is Lucas?"

Valerie helped her father rise back up from the floor. She noticed that he was beginning to tremble a great deal.

In a soothing voice, Valerie introduced her friends to her father as they gathered around the rather unstable man.

Scott held out his hand toward Frank and said, "It's nice to finally meet you, Sir. I'm sorry about your daughter. I pray that everything goes well with her."

Frank shook Scott's hand and then he reached into a pocket to locate a handkerchief to wipe his forehead which had begun to perspire, profusely.

Marissa turned toward Lincoln and whispered, "Let's go see if your grandmother is allowed visitors yet, Lincoln."

Lincoln excused himself, as he followed Marissa to the nurse's station.

Dr. Kanaly walked up to Scott and said, "I'm afraid it does not look good for your little friend. The longer he remains in that coma, there is a greater chance that he may suffer some brain damage."

Scott began to feel the weight of the whole world suddenly being thrust upon his shoulders.

Valerie attempted to keep Scott from falling to the floor. She whispered to him, "This, my friend, calls for prayer."

Frank watched as his eldest daughter ushered Scott over to the corner of the waiting room.

After a few moments passed by, Frank decided to join them.

Just as he arrived, he heard his daughter say, "Oh, Lord, precious Jesus, only you can heal young Shaun. He's been through so much trauma as you very well know. He deserves to live out a long and healthy life. He has so much potential. I believe that he was destined to do great things with his life. I believe that you have a purpose for everyone. I believe, sweet Jesus, that you can heal Shaun and instill in him your precious mercy. We would all be truly blessed to witness your wondrous miracle of healing. Please, dear Lord, please bestow upon young Shaun your sweet blessings. In the name of our dear Lord, Jesus Christ, we pray. Amen."

Frank's eyes were beginning to moisten, a bit, as he attempted to wipe away at them.

"That was truly beautiful Valerie," Frank sobbed.

Chris sat upon the bridge with his feet dangling over the edge. Diana joined him and as she sat down she placed her arm around his shoulder. The rain was beginning to fall much harder.

"Who is this Lucas? " Diana called out over the pouring rain.

Chris turned toward Diana and corrected her as he said, "You mean, who was Lucas. Not who is Lucas. Lucas is dead now. It's all my fault, too. It should have been me, and not Lucas."

Diana felt Chris' mood was shifting altogether and she didn't much care for the direction in which it was going, either.

Diana decided to keep Chris talking by asking him questions. She thought that it might be a good idea to keep his mind occupied.

"How did he die, Chris?"

Chris lifted his hand to his head while he pretended to be holding a gun and then he pretended to fire the imaginary gun.

Diana cringed, as she commented, "What a way to go. I'm so sorry Chris. When did this happen?"

Chris replied, "A few days ago. He had a funeral and everything. His mother and his sister came all the way up from Florida just to go to his funeral. They couldn't be bothered with him while he was alive. But the minute he offs himself they come right away."

"That's awful! Weren't they nice people?"

Chris shrugged as he wiped away at his rain soaked hair.

Diana thought for a minute, then she asked, "Did they let you keep anything of his, Chris? I can remember when my favorite cousin died, her mother let me keep her dog, as a reminder of her."

Chris looked directly into Diana's face, which scared her, for she noticed something strange in his eyes.

"They let me read his journal that he was keeping. I didn't even know that Lucas liked to write. It sure made for some interesting reading. It was very........eye opening."

"How so?" Diana asked, as she began to feel a cold chill.

Chris stared out into the pouring rain and then he replied, "Lucas wrote something about me. I even memorized it, word for word. It goes like this, 'My ex-buddy Chris is suddenly too good to be in the presence of a bum like me. He doesn't call me anymore. He never comes by the Blarney Stone anymore. I guess he found out that my father was right all along. He figured out what a loser I am. I miss all those good times we used to have. We used to laugh and stay up all night long. Chris was always a rock in my life. He was always the one I could depend on. He used to believe in me. I can't stand betrayal!'"

Diana began to cry, as she watched Chris get to his feet. By now, Chris was beginning to cry, as he gave Diana a look of desperation and intense inner torment.

Chris threw off his jacket and Diana scrambled to retrieve it.

Chris cried out, "Can't you see? I let Lucas down. It was my fault he killed himself. I don't deserve to live. Lucas deserved to live."

Diana watched in horror as Chris began to climb up on the railing, rather unsteadily.

Chris turned toward Diana and called out, "I can't stand all this pain."

Panicking, Diana desperately searched Chris' pockets for his wallet which he kept in the inner pocket.

As she finally located it, Diana began to search it for some telephone number or something.

She felt that this was something that she couldn't handle by herself. At last, she was successful, as she removed a small white card. On the card she read, "Julia Monroe!"

Beneath the name, Diana noticed a scribbled telephone number.

As she glanced around in the pouring rain, Diana desperately sought out a telephone booth.

Suddenly, a man drove up in a white Cadillac. The driver rolled down his window and asked, "Is there anything I can help you with, Dear?"

Diana rushed over to the man and began to cry hysterically, "I need to get to a telephone booth. I've got to make a call. This is an extreme emergency. My friend over there has had too much to drink and I'm afraid he might hurt himself. Can you please take me to a phone booth?"

The man reached over and pulled out his cellular phone. He smiled and said, "I'll do you one better, Miss. It works fine. I just charged the batteries, yesterday. You can use it to call whoever you want to."

Diana thanked the man, as she reached for the phone. Nervously, she dialed the phone.

After several intense seconds passed by, Diana heard a voice on the other end.

"Hello," the voice said groggily.

"You don't know me," Diana began. "Is this Julia?"

Julia replied, "Yes! Who are you?"

Diana cried, "I'm Diana. Are you friends with a guy named Chris?"

Julia replied, "Yes. What's wrong with him?"

Diana screamed, as she glanced over toward Chris, who was now weaving back and forth, as he stood atop the bridge railing.

"What is it, Diana?" Julia cried out.

"He's going to jump, I think!" Diana cried.

Julia became fully alert, as she struggled to make sense of this conversation.

"Where are you, now, Diana? Please calm down and tell me where you and Chris are."

Diana began to hyperventilate a bit, as she struggled to relay her location to Julia.

After ascertaining their whereabouts, Julia spoke calmly and said, "Keep him occupied, Diana. I'll be right there."

Diana thanked the man for the use of his telephone, as she handed it back to him.

The man asked, "Would you like for me to talk to him Miss?"

"Please Sir," Diana begged. "I don't know what to do. His name is Christian."

Diana watched the man get out of his car. He was dressed in a strange white suit, which seemed to glow in the darkness which completely surrounded them.

Diana watched the man walk across the bridge directly up to where Chris stood, wavering to and fro.

Diana slowly followed the man and when she came within earshot, she heard the man say, "Christian? Is that your God given name, Son?"

Chris nodded, as he stared at the glowing figure.

"You don't want to do this, Son. Satan is attempting to corrupt you, Christian. You must find your inner strength and fight this evil before he gains his treacherous victory over your very soul. You must pray to our Heavenly Father to release from you all of this pain and torment that the devil is inflicting upon you."

Chris began to cry more and more, as he struggled to fight the evil within.

Diana placed her head into her hands, as she wept, silently. The rain began to fall heavier. With her face covered Diana could hear the man continue, "Our precious Lord feels your pain, Son. He wants to help you. All you need to do is, ask him. Knock and he shall answer."

Diana noticed that the man had ceased speaking. She removed her hands from her face, and she was completely bewildered when she noticed that the man was nowhere in sight.

She glanced back toward the spot where he had parked his white Cadillac. She felt disoriented again because the car was no longer there.

"Chris," Diana called out. "What happened to that man? He was here one minute and the next, he was gone."

Chris began to climb down off of the railing, and he replied, "I think he was an angel."

Diana felt a cold chill run down her spine.

Julia dialed a telephone number that Chris had given to her. It was Lincoln's pager number.

Julia had accepted it, thinking at the time, that there would most likely never be a time when she would ever actually have to use it.

Just as Lincoln's pager was sounding, Valerie dropped to her knees trembling slightly.

"What is it, Val?" Scott asked.

"It's Chris. Something's wrong with Chris. He needs us," Val replied.

Lincoln announced, "I'm not sure but I think Julia just paged me."

Scott rushed Lincoln over to a telephone and urged him, "Call her, Lincoln. Val has just had another one of her premonitions."

Lincoln reached Julia and asked her, "What's going on Julia?"

Julia explained, "I'm afraid that Chris is in a lot of trouble. He needs us right now. Please come to the bridge on West Rosedale. It's urgent. I think Chris is in bad shape."

Scott watched, nervously, as Lincoln's expression turned from confusion to sheer concern.

"Come on you guys," Lincoln called out. "Chris is at the bridge on Rosedale."

Julia arrived on the scene first. The rain was now coming down in torrents, as she climbed out of her car. Diana ran up to Julia. She was still crying hysterically.

"Are you, Julia?"

Julia nodded her head and urged Diana to take her to Chris.

Diana explained, "He was all right for awhile. This guy drove up in this Cadillac. I called you from his car phone. He offered to talk to Chris. Whatever he said, seemed to get through to Chris. But it didn't last. A few minutes after this guy disappeared, Chris climbs back up on the bridge railing. We've got to get him down from there. He's scaring the you know what out of me."

Julia approached Chris carefully. Just as Diana had said Chris had climbed back onto the railing, where he was trying to balance himself, dangerously.

"Chris," Julia attempted to call out soothingly, "It's me. It's Julia. Are you all right, Chris?"

Chris managed to give Julia an awkward sideways glance.

"Julia," Chris moaned. "What are you doing out here in the rain? You're getting soaked to the bone."

Julia managed a laugh as she said, "And I suppose you're not getting wet, Chris?"

Chris looked directly up towards the sky and shouted, "I love the rain. I always did. When Lucas and I were kids, we always played outside in the rain. One time we made this raft. We used this old wood that was piling up behind my father's house to build it. One time we had this really bad storm. Tornado warnings were posted and everything. Well, that didn't stop old Lucas and me from sneaking out of our houses. We took that raft that we made together, and we dragged it all the way down to Freeman's Lake. There we were, with lightning striking all around us. It was truly awesome. We completely defied Mother Nature, as we sailed our raft down the lake. We pretended to be Sinbad the sailor and Tom Sawyer, sailing down the mighty Mississippi, together. I always wanted to be Sinbad, but Lucas always got his own way."

Julia began to look around nervously, while Chris continued to babble, incessantly.

Diana squealed, "Here comes another car."

Chris squinted his eyes in the direction of the car, as it came to a halt.

"Hey," Chris called out. "That's Lincoln's car. What's he doing here?"

Lincoln quickly climbed out of his car. He was followed by Scott and Valerie.

Chris laughed hysterically, which almost sent him over the edge of the bridge, down to the water below.

"My, my," Chris giggled. "The gang's all here."

Valerie called out, "Chris, what are you doing?"

Chris called back, "I'm paying homage to a fallen comrade, Fraulein!"

Scott approached Chris carefully. He reached out to him and said, "Come on now, Chris. You don't need to be up there. Why don't you climb down and let us help you?"

Chris laughed, once again as he said, "I don't need anyone's help. I can do this perfectly well on my own, thank you very much."

Lincoln approached Chris quietly and he placed himself in a position so that Chris was able to see his face.

"Hey, Lincoln, my old buddy," Chris began. "How's it going? Where's that guitar of yours? Did you bring it, Buddy? Could you play me a tune, Lincoln?"

Lincoln continued to stare Chris down causing Chris to feel very uneasy and self conscious.

Chris began to cry softly, as Lincoln kept up the silent treatment.

"What's the matter Lincoln?" Chris asked. "Are you sore at me or something?"

Lincoln nodded his head slowly. Then in a very deep and serious tone Lincoln replied, "Chris, you dragged us all away from the hospital, where our loved ones may be dying. My grandmother is very ill. She may not live to see another sunrise. Valerie's baby sister is very ill. Scott's young friend Shaun, the one who discovered Lucas' dead body, is lying in the hospital in a coma. He may very well never live to see another sunrise either. And, here you are trying to pull a selfish stunt like this. Whatever has possessed you, Chris? Have you temporarily lost your mind? You're better than this, Man!"

Valerie noticed that Lincoln's approach was indeed getting through to Chris.

She realized that Chris may also need her tenderness and understanding. She approached Chris. Julia and Diana watched with nervous anticipation, as Valerie held out her hand toward him.

She said, "Chris, we haven't been there for you, like we should have. We should have realized what you were going through. We've all been preoccupied with ourselves. But, we're all here right now. We want to help you, Chris. We love you, Chris, very much. We need you and we do not want to lose you."

Chris' eyes failed to retain his tears any longer, as he heard the words that he was aching to hear.

Valerie immediately dropped to her knees, in fervent prayer. Scott and Lincoln continued to reach out their hands to him.

Valerie continued to pray, silently, as the rain began to fall even harder.

Julia and Diana rejoiced, as they watched Scott and Lincoln attempt to help Chris climb down from the railing. A tense moment occurred when Chris' foot slipped on the wet rail. He almost fell out of Scott's grip.

Once he was down safely, Julia ran up to Chris and wrapped her arms around his neck, crying hysterically.

Chris was beginning to sober up a bit, as he rubbed his face into Julia's warm neck.

Julia scolded her friend, "Don't you ever pull a stunt like that again Christian Johnson."

Chris laughed, "All right, Julia Monroe!"

Valerie watched with delight as Chris and Julia held each other tightly.

Valerie whispered under her breath, "Praise God!"

Chris whispered into Julia's ear, "How about it, Julia?"

Julia whispered, "How about what?"

Chris whispered, "Did you hear what Valerie said?"

Julia nodded, "Yes?"

Chris asked once again, "How about it, Julia? Do you love me, too?"

Julia giggled nervously, "Yes, but not when you do crazy things like this."

Lincoln clapped his hands together, and announced, "All right, everyone. Once again, our good Lord has persevered over Satan. We can all stand out here in the pouring rain giving him just thanks and appreciation, thus opening ourselves up to possible cases of pneumonia, or we can all pile ourselves into our nice warm cars and return to the hospital."

"To the hospital!" Chris shouted.

"To the hospital!" The others joined in, as they all ran to their cars.

As Chris and Julia neared Julia's car, Diana stopped them and announced, " I don't live far from here. I'll just walk home. I don't mind the rain, really."

Julia asked, "Are you sure? We'll drop you off."

"No thanks!" Diana said, while she held her head down in shame. "I kind of feel like this was all my fault. I supplied Chris with the liquor. I didn't realize how vulnerable he was at the time."

Chris placed his hand upon Diana's cheek. He smiled warmly and said, "Don't blame yourself, Diana. Actually, you saved me from becoming completely unglued. You called for help. You, my dear, have been a miracle waiting to happen."

Diana blushed slightly and then she almost swooned, as Chris placed a warm kiss upon her cheek.

Chris whispered, "Thank you, very much. I'll never forget what you did for me."

Diana watched as Chris and Julia slipped into their car.

Valerie asked Lincoln to wait a minute, as she climbed back out of his car. Lincoln watched as Valerie approached Diana and asked her, "Excuse me! What is your name?"

She answered, "Diana."

Valerie introduced herself and then she asked, "Have you ever heard of a church called, 'The Church of Faith in Christ'?"

Diana nodded, that she had heard of it and that she even knew where it was located.

Valerie handed Diana a small card with the times of the services listed on it.

"You are more than welcome to attend. You can sit with us. We'll look for you on Sunday."

Diana stared at the card as if she had just been handed a golden invitation to visit the Queen of England. She watched as Valerie headed back for Lincoln's car.

Diana called out, "Thanks! I......I'll....be there."

Valerie turned to face Diana, once more and then she called out, "God bless!"

Diana watched as the two cars sped off in the direction of the hospital. The rain began to subside a bit.

CHAPTER SIX

HEAVENWARD

As Valerie, Lincoln and Scott reentered the emergency waiting room, Scott immediately spotted Shaun's mother sitting in a wheelchair. She looked ghostly pale.

"Margie!" Scott ran over to the woman and then he knelt down to get a better look at her.

"Oh, Scott," Margie cried. "They prodded and they poked, and then they poked and they prodded. I feel like a human pin cushion. They won't even let me go see my boy."

"They won't let me go see Shaun, either," Scott complained.

Lincoln noticed that Marissa was missing. At the same time, Valerie failed to see her father anywhere in the waiting room.

"Where could they be?" Lincoln wondered aloud.

Once Frank had learned that Lincoln's grandmother was allowed visitors, he joined Marissa in MaryFaye's room.

"Frank, is that you?" MaryFaye asked as she attempted to focus her eyes. "Lord, it's been ages. How are you, Frank?"

Frank smiled down at his old friend, "Oh, I guess I've seen better days, MaryFaye."

Marissa smiled, "I didn't know you two were old friends."

MaryFaye smiled warmly, as she gazed upon Frank's careworn face.

"How's that little girl of yours, Frank? I hear you and your new wife had a daughter."

Frank's smile disappeared, as he explained, "I'm afraid, MaryFaye, that Faith is deathly ill. She's right here in the hospital. They won't let me see her, yet."

MaryFaye smiled, "Tell them to bring her to me, Frank."

Frank looked a little bit puzzled at MaryFaye's request.

"Go ahead, Frank. Tell them that you want to bring her in here. They'll let you if you simply ask them to."

Frank looked questioningly toward Marissa, who just simply shrugged her slender shoulders.

Marissa turned back toward MaryFaye, after Frank hurried out of the room and asked, "What are you up to, Mrs. MacWilliams?"

MaryFaye smiled warmly toward the ceiling and answered, "I'm just doing the Lord's will Child. That's all."

Erik's plane landed late that same evening. As he disembarked from the plane, he held on to the small hand of his son, Tyler. The boy looked as if he were suffering from a mild case of jet lag.

After they reached the baggage department, Tyler indicated to his father that he was hungry. Erik picked up his bag from the carousel.

"Son, we can grab something on our way to see your mother. The judge will be sentencing her, tonight."

Innocently Tyler asked, "Is she pretty Dad?"

Erik thought for a minute and then he answered, "Yes, Tyler, she is very pretty, and she's also very brave."

"Like Wonder Woman?" Tyler giggled as they spotted his bag coming up the carousel.

Erik laughed and said, "Yes, Tyler, like Wonder Woman."

Maggie faced her husband who sat across from her in a small room. A female guard stood in the corner, pretending not to be eavesdropping.

"The judge's verdict will be handed down soon, Mark. I hope Erik can get my son here before the judge reads it to me."

Mark took his wife's trembling hand in his, as he attempted to keep her calm.

"Would you like to pray, Maggie?"

Maggie nodded her head, eagerly.

As they both closed their eyes and folded their hands in humble obedience, Maggie began, "Dear Lord. I come to you out of concern for my young son. A boy whom I have never gotten a chance to get to know. After all these years I finally have the chance to see my beautiful boy, face to face. I am truly sorry for the things I've done. I am truly sorry for all of the lies I told in order to keep my secrets hidden. My whole life has been one lie after another. For the first time I can look at my husband and see the treasure I've had in him. I feel alive for the first time. Whatever sentence is handed down to me, I know I'll deserve. All that I ask for is to be able to see my son. I want to feel his arms around my neck. I want to hear him call me, Mother."

Mark noticed that his wife was beginning to lose control of her emotions, so he took over for her.

"Lord, as you know, Maggie has dealt with her alcoholism. She has admitted to everyone that she has a drinking problem. Together, with the help and support of her friends and family, I believe that you, Lord, can help her cope. Please touch the heart of the Judge as he renders his decision. Please show him how to be forgiving and compassionate. Above all else, please allow him to come to a fair and just decision. Not just for my sake or for Maggie's sake, but most importantly, for Tyler's sake. In Jesus' name we pray, Amen."

Maggie wiped the tears from her eyes as she gazed lovingly, into Mark's moistened eyes.

Valerie walked through the corridors of the pediatric wing, searching for her father reportedly, had gone up there. Moments later she spotted him at the other end, near the elevators.

He was pushing a wheelchair. In the wheelchair, sat Valerie's sister, Faith.

Valerie, quietly, sprinted toward her father.

"Daddy, what on earth, are you doing?"

Faith spoke up hoarsely, "We're going to see some nice lady that Daddy knows. She's sick, too. We're going to cheer her up."

Valerie noticed that a tear in the corner of her father's right eye was beginning to form, involuntarily, as he nodded slowly.

Valerie placed a hand over her mouth, as she realized what the look on her father's face was indicating.

Faith took Valerie by the hand, and said, comfortingly, "It's going to be all right, Valerie."

Valerie squeezed the little girl's hand. Then she knelt down and kissed it. Tears began to fall rapidly down Valerie's face, despite every effort on her part, to hold them back.

"You can come with us, Valerie," Faith offered.

Valerie looked up toward her father. He slowly nodded his head. A single tear fell from his right eye. It fell all the way down to his chin.

A doctor approached Margie and Scott, as they headed for the cafeteria.

Margie introduced the man to Scott, and then she asked, "What is it, Dr. Germaine?"

The small man, with horn rimmed glasses, replied, "I think you had better brace yourself, Mrs. Collins."

"What's wrong with Margie, Dr. Germaine?" Scott asked out of deep concern.

The doctor sat down beside Margie, took her small, thin hand in his. He began to explain, "I don't know how else to tell you this, Mrs. Collins, other than to give it to you straight."

Margie managed a nervous laugh, as she urged the doctor to get on with it.

The doctor whispered, "I'm afraid, my dear, that you have a case of full blown aids."

Margie stared into the doctor's gray eyes as if she were in a sort of trance.

Scott squeezed Margie's hand tightly, as he asked the doctor, "Are you sure, Doctor? Couldn't there have been some mistake?"

The doctor shook his head as he replied, "There's been no mistakes. I performed the tests myself."

Margie continued to stare out into blank space, as if she were in shock.

Dr. Germaine stood up and then he asked Margie, "Do you have any questions, Mrs. Collins?"

Margie nodded her head, slowly, and then she asked, "When can I see my son?"

The doctor feared, at first, that Margie may be in the initial stages of denial, but then he assumed that she might be exhibiting normal maternal instincts.

"You'll have to see Dr. Kanaly for that answer. Now, if you'll excuse me, I have other emergencies to tend to. Again, excuse me."

Scott gave Margie a comforting hug while she continued to stare in dumbfounded disbelief.

Helen arrived at the prison precisely at the same time that Rosemary Harrison and Peggy Washington arrived.

"I guess you're here for the same reasons that we're here," Peggy Washington greeted Helen.

"Yes," Helen nodded. "I came to pray for Maggie and Mark."

Rosemary gave Helen a hug and asked, "How have you been holding up, Girl?"

Helen replied, "I won't lie to you, Ladies. It's been difficult at times. But Samantha and I had a good, strong, loving relationship. I don't regret anything. She knew how much I loved her."

Peggy hugged Helen and whispered, "Keep the faith, Helen. You can always turn to Jesus for comfort."

Just as the three women were about to enter the prison, a cab pulled up to the curb. They all three stopped in their tracks and watched the passengers disembark.

"Erik!" Helen exclaimed. "Who have we here?"

Erik presented his son to the ladies, proudly. He said, "Ladies, this here, is Tyler Masterson. He's come here to meet Maggie, his mother, for the first time."

Helen extended her hand to the small boy.

"I'm pleased to meet you, Tyler Masterson. I hope you can call me Aunt Helen."

"Aunt Helen?" Tyler asked. "Are you my mother's sister?"

"We're sisters in the Lord, Dear," Helen smiled warmly.

Tyler nodded his head, politely, as he said, "Oh!"

The three women laughed in unison, as they all entered the prison.

Mark was informed by a guard that Maggie's son had just arrived. He quickly rose from his seat, squeezed Maggie's hands reassuringly, and then he left the room to get the boy.

Maggie quietly sat in her seat. The seconds that ticked away seemed like an eternity.

Suddenly she jumped. The quiet solitude was interrupted by the opening of the door.

A small boy entered the room. He was acting a bit frightened and overwhelmed.

Maggie sat at the huge wooden table just staring, lovingly, at the small boy. A smile ran across her face as she recognized certain family traits that the boy possessed. Maggie realized that the boy had her mother's eyes, and her father's nose. She laughed, softly, as she recognized the fact that Tyler had been blessed with Erik's thick black hair.

"Come here, Tyler. Let me hug my big boy."

Tyler sheepishly approached Maggie. He had buried his hands deep into his trouser pockets, as he walked up to the woman wearing prison clothes.

Maggie hugged Tyler so tightly, he was forced to remove his hands from his pockets. Instinctively, he wrapped his arms around her neck.

Maggie cried, "You've grown into quite a big little man, Tyler. Tell me about yourself. What do you like to do?"

Tyler shrugged his shoulders and replied, " I mostly I like to play with my dog and fly kites and go fishing."

Maggie sat Tyler up on her knee. She asked him, "What kind of dog do you have, Tyler?"

Tyler replied, "I have a collie. I wanted to get a german shepherd, but when I saw Callie at the pet store, I knew that I had to get her."

"That's cute!" Maggie laughed.

Outside of the room where Maggie and Tyler were getting acquainted, Mark had assembled Helen, Rosemary, Erik and Peggy. He asked them to join hands with him as he led them in prayer. Mark prayed, "Dear Lord. The judge is now about to reach his decision. We pray for justice to be served in this most unfortunate case, in which my wife is involved. We pray that, above all else, that your will be done. Whatever decision is rendered, we pray that Maggie will be able to deal with it, in a way that is pleasing to you, Lord."

Peggy prayed, "Dear Lord. Precious Jesus. I have found it in my own heart to forgive Maggie for causing this tragedy. It's affected so many lives. It's true that I miss my daughter, Denise. There is nothing on this earth that can ever replace the aching, the emptiness in my heart caused by this senseless act. But, as a true believer, Lord, in your word, I know that someday, I shall be reunited with my daughter in Heaven. Please touch the heart of the judge and teach him about forgiveness. Maggie deserves a second chance."

Rosemary prayed, "Dear Lord. Maggie has just been reunited with her precious little boy. He never knew her until today. It would be so cruel and sad if they can't be together for the rest of their lives. That boy needs to get to know his mother. He needs to feel her warmth and kindness. I truly believe that since all of Maggie's secrets have been exposed that she has truly learned her lesson. I truly believe that she can handle whatever slings and arrows that Satan has up his sleeves to throw at her. I believe that Maggie is truly stronger, now."

Erik took in a deep breath, exhaled quickly, and prayed, "Dear Lord. I come to you, humbly and full of shame. I am not completely blameless in all of this. It's true that I am not responsible for the deaths of Denise and Adam. I am equally to blame for all of the pain and suffering that Maggie has been experiencing, all of these years. I kept Tyler away from her, as was her request, but I encouraged her to go on keeping our little secret for my own selfish reasons. I had become engaged to Samantha Taylor and I knew that if the existence of Tyler were made public, it may have presented many complicated problems for everyone involved. Two years ago, Maggie had a change of heart. She wanted me to bring Tyler here to live with her. She was ready to confess everything to her husband. I talked her out of it, so I could keep the truth from reaching Samantha. Well, now, Samantha has been taken away from us, too. I guess there's a valuable lesson here. There are many valuable lessons here. Please help me to be more honest with others as well as with myself. Not for my sake, but primarily, for the sake of my son, Tyler."

Mark prayed, "Lord! You taught us this prayer."

All five joined in unison after Mark led, "The Lord is my shepherd; I shall not want. He maketh me to lie down in green pastures: he leadeth me beside still waters. He restoreth my soul: he leadeth me in the paths of righteousness for his name's sake. Yea, though I walk through the valley of death, I will fear no evil: for thou art with me; thy rod and thy staff they comfort me. Thou preparest a table before me in the presence of my enemies: thou anointest my head with oil; my cup runneth over. Surely goodness and mercy shall follow me all of the days of my life: and I will dwell in the house of the Lord forever.

Amen."

Judge Oliver J. Youngblood had been deliberating over Maggie Jenner's drunken driving case. He had arrived at a decision, however, he was beginning to have second thoughts. It seemed that his conscience was getting the better of him, as he was about to summon the interested parties to his chambers so that he could render his decision. The judge realized that the dramatic reading of the confession by Maggie Jenner herself, had indeed, affected him to a certain degree. However, he also realized that he was not to be swayed by emotions. He was sworn to judge Mrs. Jenner fairly. After all, the honorable judge realized that if Maggie Jenner were to be set free and if she were to commit the exact same offense, the public outcry would be to have his head placed firmly upon a platter.

The judge decided to further deliberate before rendering his final decision.

Valerie and Frank smiled as they entered MaryFaye's room, with Faith in tow. They found Lincoln and Marissa sitting at the foot of the bed laughing along with the elderly woman.

"What's this!" MaryFaye exclaimed. "Who is this beautiful young child! It's so nice to see such an angelic face in this gloomy place."

Faith took an instant liking to MaryFaye, as she struggled to climb out of the wheelchair.

"No," Frank warned. "Faith, you mustn't exert yourself."

Faith sat back down in her chair. She let out a sigh of frustration, as she told her father, bluntly, "Daddy, I know it and the doctors know it. I can see it in your eyes and I can even see it in Valerie's eyes. We all know that I am going to die, soon. Why can't I exert myself enough to give this lady a great big sloppy kiss and a hug?"

MaryFaye laughed so hard, that it worried Marissa and Lincoln, as they looked on with concern.

Valerie and Frank reluctantly, allowed Faith to rise out from her chair, with their help.

MaryFaye motioned for Faith to lie in her arms beside her. Faith turned and gave MaryFaye a kiss on the cheek.

MaryFaye laughed, "Thank you, precious child."

Faith smiled up at the woman and then she nuzzled her face into MaryFaye's neck.

MaryFaye announced, "This was the purpose that the good Lord had in mind for me. He wanted me to hang around long enough to meet this beautiful young girl."

Lincoln smiled at the sight of Valerie's little sister in his grandmother's arms. He had never seen his grandmother look so much at peace before.

After getting over the shock of the news that was given by Dr. Germaine, Margie and Scott insisted that they be able to see Shaun.

Reluctantly, the doctor decided to allow them entrance to the intensive care unit, where Shaun lie completely motionless.

Margie began to cry silently, as they neared Shaun's bed. He looked ghostly pale. He was hooked up to a heart monitor and a breathing apparatus. There was a catheter beside his bed also.

"He looks so helpless," Margie cried.

Scott held Margie up in order to prevent her from collapsing. He shook his head solemnly, for it did not look good for his unfortunate little friend.

Scott whispered, "Sit down here, Margie," as he indicated a chair.

Margie whispered, "What are you doing, Scott?"

Scott got down on his knees and began to pray silently, while Margie looked on.

Judge Youngblood, after careful deliberation, gathered everyone concerned into his chambers.

Mark sat beside his wife holding her hand, tightly. Tyler sat on the other side of Maggie holding onto her other hand, tightly. His tiny face seemed to beam with childlike innocence.

Erik stood behind his son, with one hand on his shoulder.

Helen held onto Erik's right hand, which sort of gave him a connection with Samantha, whose presence he thought was, somehow, being felt.

Peggy Washington held onto Helen's other hand, which Helen was very grateful for, while, Rosemary Harrison placed her arm around Peggy's waist tightly, as everyone realized that Maggie's moment of truth had, at long last arrived.

Judge Youngblood looked into the faces of everyone assembled before him. He first gazed into the eyes of the mothers of the young couple who were forced off of the road into a tree by Maggie. They both appeared to have found some sort of inner peace with the whole ordeal.

He then looked into the eyes of Helen as she comforted the father of Maggie's illegitimate child. This man had been engaged to this woman's daughter, who had recently died from a gunshot wound.

The judge then gazed directly into Erik's eyes and he noticed shades of guilt in them, as he had the tendency to look away from his gaze. The judge's eyes came to rest upon the sweet, innocent face of Maggie's little boy. The boy either was completely ignorant of what was transpiring before him, or the child simply had more self confidence than anyone else in the room.

As Judge Youngblood skipped over Maggie, in order to save her for last, his eyes came to rest upon the face of Maggie's husband. His loyalty to his wife was remarkable to the judge.

He had never, in all of his years on the bench, had ever seen so much blind trust and loyalty toward one's spouse. He watched how Mark held tightly to his wife despite all of the pain and suffering she had caused so many people. Despite all of her treachery, Mark still obviously loved his wife very much.

Judge Youngblood's eyes came to rest upon Maggie, herself. He saw how the reunion with her son had sparked some sort of renewed sense of spirit within her. He spotted a peculiar, joyous twinkle in her eyes.

Judge Youngblood cleared his throat and announced, "I have reached my verdict. I find Maggie Jenner guilty of involuntary manslaughter while driving under the influence of alcohol. That should come as no surprise to anyone assembled here. It is the opinion of the court that Maggie Jenner must pay for her crime. She has although expressed true regret and remorse for what she has done. Of that, I am not doubtful.

I sentence Maggie Jenner to two years in jail, for the crime she has admitted to was by no means premeditated. I order Maggie Jenner to obtain counseling for her alcohol addiction. Following her two year sentence in the county jail, I am placing her on ten years probation. She shall report to a probation officer once a week. I want the court to have complete assurance that she remains clean. As for her visiting rights, I am allowing her husband and her son all of the visits that they wish for. It is not the will of this court to keep mother and child separated for any more length of time than has already been lost. An officer of the court shall escort Mrs. Jenner back to her cell immediately."

Everyone arose as Judge Youngblood struck his gavel upon his desk and then he left the room.

Maggie hugged Rosemary and Peggy, thanked them for coming and for their prayers and support. She then tearfully hugged Helen and said, "I'm so sorry about Samantha. She was a lovely woman."

Maggie hugged Erik and thanked him for bringing Tyler to see her in time.

Maggie tearfully hugged Mark, and whispered, "If you don't want to wait two years Mark, I'll understand. You can have our marriage annulled."

Mark cried uncontrollably, "Nonsense Honey. I'll stick by you no matter what."

Maggie couldn't hold back the tears, as she picked up her son, who refused to shed a tear.

"It's all right to cry, Tyler," Maggie whispered.

Tyler said proudly, "Big boys don't cry. Besides, that old judge said that I could come and visit you any old time I want to."

Maggie glanced over at Erik and cried, "He's so precious."

Suddenly, a guard entered the room and grabbed Maggie by the elbow and motioned for her to place Tyler down.

Maggie's heart seemed to skip a beat or two as she relinquished her hold upon Tyler.

The guard began to lead Maggie out of Judge Youngblood's chambers to begin serving her two year sentence. Just before she lost sight of Tyler, Maggie noticed that the little boy's eyes had begun to water.

After Marissa, Valerie and Frank left the room for a little while, MaryFaye looked over at her grandson who was still seated at the foot of her bed.

"You know you're going to have to decide, Lincoln."

Faith smiled up at MaryFaye as if she knew exactly what the elderly woman was talking about.

Lincoln asked, "Decide? About what, Gram'?"

MaryFaye smiled warmly, "You know what I'm talking about young man."

Lincoln shook his head. "No, Gram'! You can't be referring to Valerie or Marissa."

MaryFaye and Faith both nodded their heads in unison, with broad smiles across their faces.

Lincoln laughed, "I think that I'll leave you two matchmakers alone for awhile. Why don't you sing to Faith, Gram'? I think she'll probably enjoy it."

MaryFaye and Faith both watched Lincoln exit the room.

MaryFaye whispered, with a slight giggle, "I thought he'd never leave."

Faith giggled softly, as she shifted her weight a bit, while lying in MaryFaye's warm arms.

"Are you comfortable, Child?" MaryFaye asked.

Faith nodded with a smile.

MaryFaye thought for a moment and then she began to sing, "Jesus loves the little children, all the little children of the world. Red, yellow, black and white. They are precious in his sight. Jesus loves the little children of the world."

Faith laid her head against MaryFaye's head and she whispered, "Sing some more, MaryFaye."

Scott rose from a deep sleep. He had accidentally fallen asleep while sitting in the chair that Margie had been sitting in, earlier.

Margie laughed, "Well, look who finally woke up."

Scott gently scolded Margie, "Why on earth did you let me fall asleep?"

Margie laughed, once again, "Well, excuse me, but you obviously needed it. You ought to be thanking me, instead of scolding me. Shaun hasn't stirred one bit. Poor kid."

Scott yawned, stretched his legs, and then stood up. He stepped over toward Shaun's bed.

"He looks so much at peace," Scott observed.

"I miss him already," Margie cried.

"Oh, don't start any of that negative talk, Margie," Scott chastised her. "He's going to make it. I know he will."

Margie rubbed her hands along her frail arms and whispered, "I wish I could be as optimistic as you are, Scotty."

MaryFaye noticed that the moon was visible outside of her hospital window.

"Look, Faith!" MaryFaye shouted, just as she noticed that Faith was about to doze off, "It's a full moon tonight. Isn't it beautiful?"

Faith squinted her eyes, and then she spotted the luminescent moon.

"It's lovely!" Faith murmured.

MaryFaye began to hum a little bit, and then she smiled as Faith joined in the humming.

"Do you know that song, Faith?" MaryFaye asked.

Faith started singing softly, "He's got the whole world in his hands. He's got the whole wide world in his hands. He's got the whole world in his hands. He's got the whole world in his hands."

MaryFaye continued the song, while Faith closed her eyes, with a contented smile on her face.

MaryFaye sang, "He's got the little bitty babies in his hands. He's got the little bitty babies in his hands. He's got the little bitty babies in his hands. He's got the whole world in his hands. He's got you and me sister in his hands. He's got you and me brother in his hands. He's got you and me sister in his hands. He's got you and me brother in his hands. He's got the whole world in his hands."

Faith roused a little from a drowsy slumber, as she looked around, "Oh, yeah!" she laughed.

MaryFaye asked, "What's the matter, Child? Did you forget where you were for a second?"

Faith asked MaryFaye, "Do you believe in Heaven, MaryFaye?"

MaryFaye replied, "Of course I do, Faith. Don't you?"

Faith nodded as she said, "All children go to Heaven. My Sunday school teacher told us that, last summer. That means I'll get to see my mother, soon. I can't wait. I miss her so much."

"How did she die, Faith?" MaryFaye asked.

Faith answered, "She was killed by a drunk driver."

MaryFaye's eyes began to glisten, as she felt Faith's pain and loss.

"You're a very brave little girl, Faith," MaryFaye praised.

Faith reached up and gave MaryFaye a big hug around the neck and then she gave her another kiss on the cheek.

Faith, once again, nestled comfortably back into MaryFaye's arms.

MaryFaye began to sing softly, "Silent night. Holy night. Shepherds quake at the sight. Round yon virgin mother and child. Sleep in heavenly peace. Sleep in heavenly peace."

In the middle of this latest song Frank, Valerie, Marissa and Lincoln reentered the room.

The sight of his daughter resting comfortably in MaryFaye's arms, pleased Frank to no end.

Faith attempted to open her eyes, as she asked, "MaryFaye what do you think Heaven will be like?"

MaryFaye smiled over toward Frank and Valerie, who realized that Faith was not even aware that they were standing there.

"I think there will be an awful lot of singing and laughing going on. Everyone will love one another. There will be no more sickness, no more war, no more fighting. Heaven is going to be a beautiful place, Faith."

Faith opened her mouth to say something, when all of a sudden she arched her back and fell into a slump. Calmly, while the others looked on, MaryFaye felt for the little girl's pulse. MaryFaye smiled serenely.

She announced, "Faith is now in Heaven with her mother."

Frank turned toward Valerie and buried himself in her arms, and sobbed uncontrollably.

Lincoln reached out to take the little girl from MaryFaye's grasp, but she stopped him.

"No, Lincoln. Leave her be."

Lincoln backed away slightly, as he watched his grandmother close her eyes.

MaryFaye began to hum the tune, 'Jesus loves the little children.'

As Lincoln and the others looked on, MaryFaye placed a hand upon her heart and she smiled despite the pain of another attack. The final words on MaryFaye's lips were, "Sweet precious Jesus."

Pastor Mark addressed his congregation. He said, "I want to thank you all for coming to this very special service, this morning. I know that a few of you have had extremely rough times, lately. Some of you have been up all hours of the night. Today's service will not be long. As many of you no doubt know, my dear wife has been sentenced to prison for two years. I will stand by her, as she goes through this trying time. I know that our precious Savior shall comfort her in her time of need.

"We have lost a very dear friend, last night. It is my understanding that she joined our Heavenly Father, rather peacefully during the night. I am, of course, referring to MaryFaye MacWilliams. She was a dear friend to us all and she will be truly missed. She is probably up there in Heaven, singing praises to our Lord, Jesus Christ. She was truly a treasure.

"Sister Valerie has also suffered the loss of her young half sister. Faith, as it happens, died in the arms of MaryFaye, herself, just mere minutes before she passed on. Our condolences go out to Lincoln, Valerie and to Valerie's father, Frank. I understand that we have some visitors here, this morning. Would you please stand up, young lady, and introduce yourself?"

Diana stood up, as Valerie held onto her trembling hand, and said, "My name is Diana Woods. Valerie invited me here today. I witnessed a miracle yesterday, and I was so glad to be invited to come to church. No one has ever invited me to church before. I just wanted to come here, today, to thank God, personally."

"You are always welcome to come here, Diana. We are a very friendly church and you'll find that we all love one another just as it was commanded of us to do, by our Lord Jesus Christ."

Diana was about to sit down when Alice stood up and gently asked Diana to come forward with her.

Diana looked puzzled, but she obliged Alice, as she followed her to the altar.

Alice held onto Diana's hand, as she began to speak to the congregation, "Last Sunday, I received the blessings of the Holy Ghost, as I received Jesus Christ as my Lord and personal Savior. Up until last Sunday, my life was mired in all kinds of filth. I too, witnessed a miracle, last week. My baby was kidnapped by a crazed man who has probably fled the country. He may never receive his punishment here on earth, but I am sure, unless he repents, he shall receive his just rewards in the hereafter. Diana has been brought here for a reason. That reason is so that she could hear the gospel. I believe everything happens for a reason. Whatever the circumstances are, that have brought her here, are entirely her business. But, it's my prayer this morning, that she leave here a child of our most holy God."

Diana thanked Alice and as they both sat back down, Pastor Mark continued, "Thank you, Alice. You have made your point rather succinctly. So, for the benefit of Diana and whosoever else is in need of hearing the gospel, I suggest that we all turn to the Book of John, the third chapter. "There was a man of the Pharisees, named Nicodemus, a ruler of the Jews: The same came to Jesus by night, and said unto him. Rabbi, we know that thou art a teacher come from God: for no man can do these miracles that thou doest, except God be with him. Jesus answered and said unto him, 'Verily, verily, I say unto thee. Except a man be born again, he cannot see the kingdom of God.' Nicodemus, a ruler of the Jews: The same came to Jesus by night, and said unto him, Rabbi, we know that thou art a teacher come from God: for no man can do these miracles that thou doest, except God be with him. Jesus answered and said unto him, 'Verily, Verily, I say unto thee, Except a man be born again, he cannot see the kingdom of God.' Nicodemus saith unto him, How can a man be born when he is old? can he enter the second time into his mother's womb, and be born? Jesus answered, 'Verily, verily, I say unto thee, Except a man be born of water and of the Spirit, he cannot enter into the kingdom of God. That which is born of the flesh; and that which is born of the Spirit is spirit. Marvel not that I said unto thee, Ye must be born again. The wind bloweth where it listeth, and thou hearest the sound hereof, but canst not tell whence it cometh, and whither it goeth; so is every one that is born of the spirit.' Nicodemus answered and said unto him, How can these things be? Jesus answered and said unto him, 'Art thou a master of Israel, and knowest not these things? Verily, verily, I say unto thee, We speak that we do know, and testify that we have seen; and ye receive not our witness. If I have told you earthly things, and ye believe not, how shall ye believe, if

I tell you of heavenly things? And no man hath ascended up to heaven, but he that came down from Heaven, even the Son of man which is in heaven. And as Moses lifted up the serpent in the wilderness, even so must the Son of man be lifted up: That whosoever believeth in him should not perish, but have eternal life. For God so loved the world, that he gave his only begotten Son, that whosoever believeth in him should not perish, but have everlasting life. For God sent not his Son into the world to condemn the world; but that the world through him might be saved. He that believeth on him is not condemned: but he that believeth not is condemned already, because he hath not believed in the name of the only begotten Son of God. And this is the condemnation, that light is come into the world, and men loved darkness rather than light, because their deeds were evil. For every one that doeth evil hateth the light, neither cometh to the light, lest his deeds be reproved. But he that doeth truth cometh to the light, that his deeds may be made manifest, that they are wrought in God.'"

Diana looked up from the Bible and let out a long breath, as she whispered, "That's sure a mouthful."

Pastor Mark smiled at his congregation and they returned his smile.

"Lincoln," Pastor Mark asked, "could you come up here and play something while I give the invitation?"

Lincoln went to the front of the congregation, with his guitar in hand. As he sat down, he said, "First, Pastor Mark, if it's all right with you, I would like to play a special song as a sort of tribute to the late MaryFaye MacWilliams, my grandmother."

Pastor Mark said, "Of course, Lincoln. As you wish."

Lincoln began to strum his guitar gently. When he was comfortable with the sound, he began to play a song that his grandmother adored. He began to play, 'Joy to the World'.

After a few minutes passed by, several members of the congregation arose and began to sing along with Lincoln, while the others stood up and clapped their hands together. The entire church became filled with the love and joy that worshiping Jesus Christ brings.

After the song was finished, Pastor Mark, solemnly, announced, "Let us pray!"

A hush fell over the congregation as Pastor Mark prayed, "Dear Heavenly Father, there are several people here, today, who came to hear the reading of your word. I pray that their hearts were touched by your words, Lord. I pray that they come to the understanding that they can only be saved through you, Lord. There is no other way to find salvation. Salvation cannot be bought. It cannot be earned by doing great works. Salvation can only come to those who confess with their mouths, and truly believe with their hearts, that Jesus Christ is Lord. I pray this morning, that these people will put away all of their foolish pride. I pray that they will let you into their hearts, Lord. I pray that they will allow you to become Master over their lives. Without you Lord, their lives are shallow and meaningless. Please, Oh Lord, create in them the desire to seek you out, Lord. In the name of our precious Lord, Jesus Christ, we pray. Amen!"

Diana began to walk a bit uncertainly toward the front. She knelt before the altar.

Valerie and Alice joined her. They placed their hands upon her shoulders. Diana prayed silently.

Meanwhile, Rico placed his hands over his face and began to cry. Chris noticed Rico's breakdown first, so he walked over toward him and sat down beside him.

Chris whispered, "Are you all right, Man? Do you want to go forward?"

Rico nodded his head, and as he attempted to stand up, his knees buckled underneath him.

Pastor Mark raced down toward Rico and placed his hand over him.

Pastor Mark announced to everyone, "The Holy Spirit is alive and well this morning. Brother Rico is filled with the Holy presence of our dear Savior, as we speak."

Chris helped Rico get to his feet, while Pastor Mark asked him, "Rico, do you believe that you are a sinner?"

Rico nodded his head.

Pastor Mark continued, "Brother Rico, do you confess with your mouth that Jesus Christ is your Lord and Savior?"

Rico managed to make it to the front of the room, where Diana was still praying silently. He turned toward the congregation, and said, "It's a miracle that I'm even here today. By all rights I should be dead. I watched a friend of mine massacre an entire room full of people. For some reason he spared me before taking his own life. I have no one else to thank for this miracle but our Lord Jesus Christ, who brought me out of the gutter and into the light. Jesus brought this precious little baby into my life, who is another miracle, himself. And, Alice, sweet Alice. He brought this wonderful angel into my life. She's been my rock, my port in the storm. Without her influence, I don't know where I would be right now. This......."

Rico cried as he watched Diana, Valerie and Alice praying silently. He continued, "This is all so..........incredible. What I'm feeling right now is all so......incredible."

Rico turned back toward Pastor Mark.

Mark walked right up to Rico, placed his hand upon his shoulder, looked him straight into the eyes, and repeated his question, "Rico, do you confess that Jesus Christ is your Lord and personal Savior?"

Suddenly, Rico felt the gentle touch of Alice's hand upon his hand. A surge of warm, loving kindness completely overwhelmed Rico, so much so, that he grabbed Alice, and gave her a hug. Both, Rico and Alice began to cry, incessantly. Rico turned back toward Pastor Mark. Still crying, he nodded his head.

With so much confidence, he said, "I sure do, Pastor Mark. I have no doubt about it. Jesus Christ is the Way, the Truth and the Life. Like you said, earlier, I believe that there is no other way. From here on out, I will trust in Jesus to guide my footsteps. Jesus Christ is most assuredly Lord."

Valerie rose to her feet and then she helped Diana rise from her knees. Diana turned toward the congregation, took one look at Rico, and started to bawl.

Rico placed his hands upon Diana's trembling shoulders, and said, soothingly, "Everything's going to be all right Diana, from here on out. You'll see. Just place your trust and your faith in Jesus, and everything will be just fine. Throw away the things of the past. Forget all of that junk in your life. You don't need those memories dragging you under. Satan can only be as powerful as you allow him to be. Accept Jesus as your own personal savior and with his help, you can conquer any demons."

Diana nodded her head as she began to wipe away at her eyes. Chris joined her up front, gave her a big hug and asked, "Are you all right, Diana?"

Diana nodded, held her head down low, and whispered into Chris' ear, "I almost caused your death yesterday."

Chris told Diana, "Hush! That's all in the past now. I was just as much to blame as anyone. Forget all of that, and turn your eyes upon Jesus. Like one of our songs say, 'Look full in his wonderful face. And the things of earth will look strangely dim, in the light of his glory and grace.'"

Diana cried, "I want to believe. But how can I be sure?"

Helen made her way to the front of the church and stood directly in front of Diana, and asked her, "Dear, is your mother still living?"

Diana shook her head.

Helen explained, "I recently lost my daughter. I was looking to unofficially adopt another one. Would you mind if I unofficially adopt you?"

Diana's eyes were refilled with tears, as Helen hugged her, sending warm love throughout her entire body. All of Diana's emotions broke lose like water through a dam. Diana let down all of the walls and barriers that she had been building over the years. Diana asked Helen, "Could you please help me to find this Jesus Christ?"

Helen smiled, imagined for a moment that Samantha was standing nearby, watching with glad spirits, as she led Diana back to the altar, where they both knelt down to pray.

Helen prayed aloud, "Dear Jesus, Diana here is the answer to my prayers. She has come into our lives, to bless us, as she seeks your face. Hers will be such a lasting testimony, one that shall affect many lives to come. She has arrived at a time when I have been missing my Samantha so sorely. You said once, that whomsoever shall hear you knocking at the door, hears you calling them, and then opens it, you shall enter in and fellowship with them. Please touch Diana's heart with the divine power of your precious Spirit. She seeks your face right now, Lord."

Suddenly, Diana collapsed, right where she had been kneeling.

Pastor Mark ran up to the front and smiled down at the young woman, as she lay there, flat on her back, looking up toward Heaven, smiling serenely.

Lincoln began to strum his guitar. Soon, everyone recognized the tune. Softly, the entire congregation began singing, "Our God is an awesome God. He reigns on Heaven and Earth. He rules with power and love. Our God is an awesome God."

After each stanza was sung, the congregation would sing the next one even louder and with much more power, as they began to feel the incredible strength behind the power of the Holy Spirit.

Meanwhile, Margie and Scott had spent the night in Shaun's room, where he had been transferred around two in the morning. The doctors were all losing their individual optimism as to whether or not Shaun would ever come out of his deep comatose condition.

Scott grabbed Margie by the hands and he began to pray, silently.

Margie began to feel extremely tired as she struggled to keep her eyes open.

Although Shaun was unable to communicate with his friend and with his mother, he was quite aware of their presence. That gave him much comfort, as he lay there, thinking.

Shaun began to imagine himself on a beach with his mother. They were gathering seashells, placing them in a small sack. They laughed in the warm sunshine and basked in their joy of just spending time with one another.

Suddenly, dark clouds appeared to Shaun. His mother, who had been standing only two feet away, suddenly disappeared. An evil sounding laughter filled the darkening sky. Shaun began to tremble. He felt an awful, evil presence surround him from all sides. The sack that he had been carrying fell to the sandy shore beneath his feet. Shaun stopped to pick up the bag. Jerking his hand back, Shaun became terrified as he watched several snakes slither out of the sack toward him, perilously. From somewhere beyond, Shaun could hear the voice of Scott as he prayed. He could only make out a word now and then. Shaun heard Scott utter the word, "Salvation", and then a few minutes later, Shaun could make out the word, "Forgiveness". Shaun ran down the beach at full force. The sun had completely disappeared behind dark clouds. Shaun felt the force of a gale wind begin to develop all around him. Shaun struggled to maintain his balance, as the wind picked up it's velocity. Again, Shaun could hear Scott's voice faintly, above the roar of the wind. This time he could make out the word, "Savior".

Shaun began to piece together the three words. He turned around and spotted a strange looking creature following him.

Shaun stopped in his tracks and marveled at the peculiar sight. The creature was beginning to close in on him. Shaun began to feel the heat from it's fiery breath. He felt powerless to escape this phenomenon.

Above the roar, Shaun distinctly heard Scott call out, with a loud voice, "Begone Satan!"

Suddenly, the creature disappeared. The sky began to brighten up, slowly. Shaun noticed the three snakes begin to shrivel up, right where they were crawling. The vision of his mother reappeared from down the beach. She was waving to him. Shaun waved back, and then he headed back toward her.

He could hear Scott much clearer now, as he made his way through the sand. Shaun could hear Scott as he said, "Thank you, Jesus. Thank you, dear Lord. Bless you sweet Jesus. Praise your name. Praise your name, Jesus."

Shaun wanted so much, to snap out of this condition so that he could speak to Scott and his mother. Frustration began to set in as Shaun lay there, helplessly.

Suddenly, everything went completely dark.

Dr. Kanaly raced into the room, alongside a nurse, when they became alarmed at the sound of Shaun's life support system.

Scott and Margie jumped out of the way. Margie watched in horror, as a flat line appeared on the small monitor.

Scott felt his heart jump through his throat.

Shaun stood in the cold darkness for what seemed like an eternity. He felt the temperature begin to plummet, rapidly. His instinct was to jump up and down to get his circulation working again, but he found that he was unable to do so.

Dr. Kanaly placed two electrodes onto Shaun's small chest. He instructed the nurse to proceed, as he yelled, "Clear!"

Shaun's body received electric volts in order to get his heart to resume beating.

Margie watched the flat line in horror, for it remained on the monitor.

Shaun squinted his eyes as he peered through the pitch blackness. Beyond, what looked to be like several yards, Shaun spotted a tiny white light. That light held a certain attraction to him.

Scott took Margie's hand in his and held onto it, tightly. Margie watched as the doctor administered the shock treatment to her son again. Scott closed his eyes and whispered, "Come on, Sweet Jesus. Please spare this boy's life."

Shaun began to walk slowly toward the light which was about the size of a soccer ball.

Dr. Kanaly swore under his breath when he realized that the second time he attempted to jump start Shaun's heart was just as unsuccessful as the first time. The nurse cried out, "We must try again!"

Shaun drew ever closer to the light. It was now apparent to him, that he was approaching a doorway.

Dr. Kanaly and the nurse tried once again. Margie found herself crossing her fingers. Scott continued to plead for Shaun's recovery.

Shaun approached the doorway. He found himself within mere inches of the entrance. A figure appeared at the door.

Dr. Kanaly turned to face Margie and Scott after they stood watching his attempt to revive Shaun fail for the third time. Dr. Kanaly removed the mask from his face and whispered, "I'm so sorry, Mrs. Collins. We did everything humanly possible."

Margie turned to Scott and cried, "It's in God's hands now."

Shaun struggled to make out the features of the figure as it stood in the doorway. He was unsuccessful in making it out. A loud, booming voice began to speak. It carried with it great authority and reverence.

Scott placed his hands upon Shaun's chest, and prayed, "Dear Lord. It's up to you, Lord. Let your will be done. Amen."

Shaun began to shake as he heard the voice announce, "Shaun, you have been through a great deal in your short life. You have experienced much. You must go forth and do the Lord's bidding. You shall do great things. You shall touch many, many lives. It is not your time to leave this world. Go forth and spread the Gospel of our Lord Jesus Christ. Go in peace."

Scott's eyes opened wide with excitement, as he began to feel Shaun's heart resume beating. Margie placed her own hands upon Shaun's chest and began to jump for joy, crying tears of incredible happiness.

Scott called out to the doctor and the nurse who had stepped out into the corridors.

"What's happened?" Dr. Kanaly asked, as he rushed into the room.

"He's alive! He's alive!" Margie cried.

"A miracle has happened, Doctor!" Scott announced proudly. "It's a miracle!"

EPILOGUE

There is no greater love than when someone lays down their life for another. God knew this and that is why He sent His own Son to live and breathe among us, just to have Him pay the ultimate price so that we may seek forgiveness and have everlasting life.

Stepping in front of a hired killer's bullet took much courage, faith and love. Everything happens for a reason. Helen survived the death threat. She, in turn, came to the aid of a lost soul who was searching for the truth.

Shaun lived out a very dangerous lifestyle in order to escape a very volatile home life.

Through Scott's constant intervention, Shaun survived imminent death. By virtue of the prayers that were spoken on his behalf, and the dreams that were delivered to him, Shaun lived to discover the truth of the gospel of Jesus Christ.

Chris learned a valuable lesson following his own reckless choices. Along the way he found love when he wasn't even aware that he'd been looking for it.

Pastor Mark gained more wisdom through the ordeal that he and his wife endured. He gained a greater understanding about forgiveness and true repentance.

Lincoln continues to ponder upon the choice that his grandmother had advised him to make. He is still awaiting an answer from the almighty Counselor Himself, Jesus Christ.

Valerie and her father overcame their painful past and have formed a bond so strong that it could never be broken, again.

ACKNOWLEDGMENTS

I would like to thank Diane Balzano for her proofreading skills. I would also like to thank Fred Balzano, Anthony Beard, Doug Jastrzebski, Jason Hunsicker, Robert Stacer and many others, who are too numerous to mention, for their encouraging words of support. I would also like to thank Wayne Richards for his support as well as for lending me his artistic talent for the cover of this book. The power of the Holy Spirit deserves all the praise. Without divine guidance this book would not have been possible.

ABOUT THE AUTHOR

Daniel Duvall currently resides in Ohio. He is the proud father of two daughters, Tiffany and Jennifer. He is an equally proud grandfather of Nathan, Mia, Brook, Brittany, Steve and Jasmine.

There are many more works of fiction to come in the future. Some books will cater, specifically, to young children. Others will be written for adult audiences.

Daniel's love for Christian based drama will be prevalent throughout all of his books. They will all have spiritual messages imbedded in them. He looks upon his love for writing as his God given purpose and ministry.

Manufactured By: RR Donnelley
Breinigsville, PA USA
June, 2010